DAMAGED SECRET DADDY

A FORCED PROXIMITY SECOND CHANCE ROMANCE

CALLIE STEVENS

1

GRAYSON

I hate traveling. Absolutely hate it. I hate the endless flights, though I don't mind the champagne in first class which I always imbibe in. It calms my nerves and I love the taste of it. I hate the hotel rooms, even though they're six-star hotels, the predictable continental breakfast with the waffle maker that I don't know how to use. It's not like I'm not grateful that I have the money to splurge to stay in luxurious hotels and take first class flights or my private jet, but it's just that it becomes... monotonous.

It's like I'm living the same day over and over, some kind of endless time loop.

"What do you expect, since you haven't gotten laid in God knows how long?" my best friend Lox said after a night out when I'd complained to him after turning down three different women.

"Why should I bother? It never lasts," I replied, and Lox snorted out a laugh.

"That's the point, Gray. It doesn't last, so you don't have to worry about it."

I remained silent. Lox didn't get it. He never would. He went through several girls a week.

Loxton didn't understand what it was like to be in love and have it all taken away from you.

I sigh heavily as I wait for everyone else in first class to get off the plane, not wanting to get caught in the hustle and bustle. I'm traveling with only a carry-on since I'll only be in town for a day, settling a deal for my family's company.

I do a lot of the legwork for my company. My father doesn't like to leave his home office, which makes it my job.

I focus on work because I learned a while ago that women are a waste of time. They're just distractions, and I don't need to be distracted. I have a plan, and that plan is what's most important to me in life. Once upon a time, I thought my life would be different. Fuller, happier, a loving one. But then...

Well, the past is in the past and I refuse to think about it.

It doesn't matter, anyway. Now I'm focused on getting out of my father's company. I want to be successful in my own right, without the nepotism of having the last name Whitlock. I'm tired of people thinking I get by without working hard.

I'm smart and I've worked my whole life to earn the position I was supposedly born into.

My best friend, Lox and I both grew up with money, but we couldn't be more different. He chooses to float along in life without pressing forward and having ambition. I don't want to just slide by in life because I grew up rich, and I want to make my own way in life, outside of my last name.

It used to be the three of us. Derek was our third amigo. The third Musketeer. But shortly after things went sour in my life five years ago, he wasn't there for me unless it was to put me down. And I couldn't stand it anymore. We never actually came to blows but it was close, so I decided I was toxic enough by myself, I didn't need "friends" like him to make me feel worse. Though he still works at my company, there is no more friendship between us.

Sometimes I miss the times it was the three of us against the world, but at least I still have Lox.

Being Grayson Whitlock isn't all it's cracked up to be. It's a lot of work, despite the lazy playboy fame attached to my name because I sometimes decide to hang out with Lox for about a half an hour. We both get the fame, but only he enjoys the prize.

I look around the airport, barely remembering the name of the town I'm in. It's somewhere in upstate New York, thousands of miles away from home.

Luckily for me, though it is snowing, it isn't too bad, and I'm able to navigate my rental car to a nearby diner because my stomach is rumbling something fierce. I haven't eaten before boarding the plane, and I'm paying for it now.

Despite all the money I grew up with, I'm not a picky eater. In fact, I prefer eating simpler, homemade cooked meals. Sometimes, little gems are hidden in the form of diners in a world of fancy restaurants that overcharge you to keep you hungry

As I wait by the counter, I look around, and it's a charming little place. There's a woman standing just a little to the back behind the counter, pleading with what appears to be the owner. I don't mean to pry, but they are close enough that their words reach my ears.

"I just need to work this shift, Barry, *please*. He'll be good. Max always sits quietly and colors in his book. Felicia always lets him stay—"

"I don't give a rat's ass what Felicia does, you can't have a kid here!" the man snarls, and I raise an eyebrow. It's none of my business but I think he's being kind of a dick.

The woman has a nice curve to her ass, I can tell that

much. I don't notice much, not anymore, when it comes to women, but I can appreciate a nice form. It reminds me of someone, but I don't want to think about it. I suppose if I let myself, any woman's figure would remind me of *her*.

Her voice adds to the illusion too, but that has to be just because it's a bit high-pitched with panic. Her hair is dark, much longer than *hers* had been, after all.

The little boy grabs my attention as he's looking up at his mother with wide eyes.

He turns my way, but he isn't looking at me, just staring into space, and I'm staring at him, at eyes that are the same color as mine. So odd, but cute.

The woman turns around, her bust much smaller than the curve of her ass, and my eyes slowly pan up to her face. I would know those warm brown eyes, her upturned nose framed by her auburn hair, anywhere. If I was blind, I feel like I could sense her, smell her perfume. She always smells like lilacs, and that hasn't changed in the past five years. It's *her*.

Somehow, I've stumbled across Lillian Brooks. How is this possible?

My eyes go to the boy again, as if some force is pulling me there, and he is still looking past me. He is holding her hand. And his eyes catch my attention as I once again notice he has the exact same blue eyes that I do. Not just the color. Now that I look at him, there is something familiar about him. Something that reminds me of...

All the air seems to go out of the room and my throat feels tight and small, like a pinhole. I can't breathe, and I think about turning and getting the hell out of there. I'm wrong. I have to be wrong. Lots of kids have blue eyes, and just because his happens to be the exact shape and shade of almost violet blue that runs in the Whitlock family...

Fuck.

"Grayson?" she whispers, and I feel like I'm going to pass out, but instead I set my jaw, keeping my eyes on the child next to her.

"Who's this young man?" I ask her, my voice booming in the small diner, and people turn to look at me. I don't care.

"Max. Maximillian," the boy says, sticking out his hand to shake mine. I shake his hand, my fingers shaking, but the boy has a firm grip. My *son* has a firm grip. Because there is no question in my mind who this little boy is.

Lillian stares at me, her full mouth open in shock, and something rolls in my stomach, making me nauseous. It's familiar, more welcome than the ache in my throat and chest when I'd first recognized my own eyes in her son's face. *My* son's face.

Anger. Rage, even, boils up inside of me, and I feel like I'm going to scream. Not only has Lillian left me heartbroken, disappeared like a ghost, she'd been *pregnant*. She's hidden it from me, and my head is spinning from the insanity of all of it.

The fact that I bumped into her here, of all places, on the last leg of my business trip, hours before I need to meet with a man who will put enough money into our company to line my father's wallet for years, seems surreal. I have a son. I have a *son*, a young man who seems polite as he smiles up at me, and God, he even shares the dimple I have in my left cheek, mirrored in his right.

"Lillian," I say firmly. "I think we need to talk."

I thank God for the rage, for the hatred I feel toward her when she closes her mouth and nods, because it's so much more welcome than the devastation I felt all those years ago.

Part of me knows, though, that you don't feel hatred for someone like that unless you used to love them.

2

LILLIAN

Being late for work hasn't helped matters, but I thought that Barry would cut me some slack. After all, he'd been working plenty of times when Max hung around for my shift. Felicia, the night manager, always lets me work with Max sitting in the corner booth, coloring.

I *need* this shift. My rent is late, and although I'm working my way up in an advertising office, it doesn't pay all the bills. Being a single mom is hard most days, but some days, it's nearly impossible.

This is not the life I would have chosen for myself or my son, but I really had no other choice. I had to leave my home, my friends, my life behind. I often dream things are different and that Max's dad is a part of our lives, but I learned he didn't really want me in his life. I was just someone to pass the time. Someone who would never measure up to him or his family. I was a fling.

So, I was forced to make a decision that broke me, and this is where it brought me.

Barry is being unreasonable and I don't know what else to do. Looking around as I think of a way to convince him, my eyes land on the last person on Earth I'd ever think would get through these doors.

Of course, after the shitty morning I've had, what else should I have expected? The universe is really having a blast at my expense today. How else can I explain coming face-to-face with my past. The one that didn't think I was enough. The one who destroyed me and forced a different version of me to reborn from the ashes.

Grayson Whitlock is staring at me in a cheap diner that barely passes the health inspection score every month. And oh God, he looks the same. So handsome, so tall. I feel like I can barely breathe.

But what is he doing here, of all places? He's a billionaire, for God's sake.

"Lillian," he says, and it sounds different than the way he used to speak to me five years ago, lilting and sweet, kissing along my jawline to wake me. It sounds... flat, somehow, devoid of any emotion. "I think we need to talk."

I know he's right. But what am I going to do? I ran away from this. From him. I had to. He was never supposed to find us. Never supposed to know. Though I always dreamed of what our lives would be like if I'd been able to share this with him, I'll never know.

I never expected to have to reveal any of this. I certainly didn't expect to have to reveal it in the diner where I pick up occasional shifts to cover bills. It's embarrassing, really.

Squaring my shoulders, I nod my head slowly, and Max accompanies us to the corner booth while Barry just stares at us.

"If you're going to sit there, you gotta buy something," Barry says gruffly, and Grayson jerks his head toward him, glaring at him. "Bring us three specials."

"Oh boy," Max cheers. "I love the special."

The special isn't very special, just a plate of sausage and two biscuits drowned in sausage gravy, but Max does love it. He eats a *lot*, just like Grayson always did. It's something he got from his father along with piercing blue eyes and that dimple in his cheek. He's the spitting image of Grayson, really, so it doesn't surprise me that Grayson knows something is amiss the second he sees us.

I take a deep breath and sit down in the booth, Max sliding in next to me and looking at Grayson, someone he has no idea is his father, with curiosity.

"What's your name?" he asks, and Grayson blinks, as if surprised.

"Grayson. Grayson Whitlock."

"I'm Maximillian Brooks," Max says proudly. "Max for short."

Grayson clears his throat, ignoring me and looking at his son in awe, watching him play with the sugar packets, and it makes my heart ache.

"Grayson," I start. I need to know what he is doing here. What he wants after all these years. But he glares at me, and I shut my mouth.

"Do you know who your father is, Max?"

My breath catches in my throat. Max has asked, of course, about his father, but I haven't gotten so far as telling him. I couldn't. And it broke my heart to deny it to him every single time.

Max shakes his head. "Mom says I don't have one."

"Is that so?" Grayson looks at me, and I swear if looks could kill, I'd be dead on the spot. "What if you did? Have a father, I mean?"

"Wow," Max breathes. "That'd be great."

"You think so?" Grayson smiles, his eyes turning back to Max. I remember that smile. As much as it takes me back, I know that things changed so much he'll never turn it to me again. I know I was right in the choice I made at the time. It was the only way. But at the same time, none of them deserved being without the other, and that will always be on me, regardless of what led to me leaving.

I never forgot Grayson. He was everything to me. But as time goes by, memories change. Now, most of the time, I think our time together is some fever dream I had. I know that he didn't feel the same way about me as I felt about him. The way I *still* feel, after all these years.

"Yeah. We could play catch and stuff. Mom's not very good at catch," Max says, looking at me from the corner of his eye as if he thinks I'll be hurt or offended by that statement.

"What if I told you that I was your father?" Grayson says, and again, my breath catches. Of course, he doesn't need any more confirmation than looking at Max. But this is too much. Too fast. What does he think he is doing? Doesn't he know this is will destroy Max when he leaves? Like it destroyed me when I was forced to leave.

Max's eyes widen, but he's smiling. "Is that true? Mom, is it true?"

I can't lie to my son. Not about anything, but especially, not about this. So, I nod slowly, not knowing what else to do, and Max goes out of the booth and jumps into Grayson's lap, just like that. Max has always been a sweet kid, accepting of all the changes we had to go through with me being a single mom and having to move around a lot, trying to escape exactly this moment.

I can see tears sparkling in Grayson's blue eyes as he slowly puts his arms around his son, and I can't fight a smile, but when he looks at me, there's nothing behind his eyes but pure rage.

"Is there somewhere we can go to speak alone?" Grayson asks, and I shake my head, swallowing hard.

"No. I couldn't find a sitter, that's why he's here with me." I gesture to my uniform.

Grayson curses under his breath and Max giggles.

"Mom says that's a bad word."

"Mom's very smart," Grayson drawls, although it doesn't sound to me like he means that in a positive way.

"I can make a few calls," I say, my voice hoarse. I wasn't able to find a sitter before my shift, but maybe I can try my best friend, Maria, again, and though she said she couldn't take Max for the whole shift, I hope that she's available to watch Max for a couple of hours, if I beg her.

I step away hesitantly, but Grayson and Max are just chatting, seemingly happy. I bite my lip as I call Maria.

"Listen," I say as soon as she answers the phone. "I need a big favor."

"I told you I really can't watch Max for a night shift, Lil, I've got a date tonight," she complains.

"I just need a couple of hours. Max's dad is in town," I say, and she goes silent on the other line.

"Max's... dad?" she asks, as if that's a foreign concept.

"Yeah. I really need you to babysit, Maria, please."

"Shit. Okay, bring him over. I'll cancel my date."

All of the air goes out of my lungs in a rush.

"Thank you, Maria. I owe you one."

I walk back over to the booth, and Max is giggling like Grayson has said something hysterical. I smile at the two of them but Grayson's smile fades when he looks at me.

"If you wait here, I'll come back after I drop Max off with a friend, and we can talk," I suggest, but before I'm even done with the sentence, Grayson is shaking his head.

"Absolutely not. What guarantee do I have that you'll

come back? I won't let you take my son again," he says in a low voice, and since Max is still giggling, he doesn't hear.

I hate the way his voice sounds, low and mean, nothing compared to the way he used to talk to me five years ago.

I nod. "Fair enough. Can you give us a ride, then? The bus doesn't run for a couple of hours."

Grayson scoffs, and I assume he's upset that I bring Max on the bus. I roll my head around on my neck, frustrated. I'm doing the best I can. A car is expensive to own and put in a garage in New York, even outside the city. Not that he would know anything about that, growing up like he did.

"As if I would let you take the bus," Grayson scoffs.

"Fine," I mutter, and Grayson follows us outside as if I'm about to sprint down the street to lose him. I guess I could because having him be so close to me again is messing with me, but with Max bouncing around and asking his father a million questions, I won't do it. And honestly. I'm not really sure I want to. I know at least part of me is happy he found us. Happy the secret is out in the open. I'm just scared what that might mean for the future.

Grayson directs us to a rental car. It's a nice one, but not as fancy as I expected. In the time that we'd known each other, Grayson hadn't exactly acted like a billionaire, so I guess I shouldn't be surprised.

Despite his disdain for me using the bus, Grayson had been pretty down to earth for someone with his background.

I remain silent except to give Grayson directions to Maria's house, and Grayson doesn't speak a word to me, either, just chatting with Max here and there about his favorite shows and video games.

My head is spinning, and I don't know which way is up. I can't believe this has happened to me, today of all days. My rent is three days late and my landlord has been texting me constantly. As if on cue, my phone buzzes in my uniform pocket, but I ignore it.

Before I take Max in the house to Maria, he leaps into the front seat to give his father a big hug, and Grayson looks at him again, like he's awestruck. It's cute, and it makes my heart soar to see how much he seems to be in wonder when he looks at Max. Pain at the decision I was forced to make years ago slices through me.

I shake my head as I walk Max to see Maria. I did the only thing I could to do at that time. I did what I thought was right. And though I know there is no excuse to keeping a father from his son, I will try to explain my reasons to Grayson. Maybe he'll understand. Maybe he'll see it my way. I don't know what he is doing here or why, but I do know that I'll never give up Max. But I also know that I won't deprive either of them from the other any longer, so maybe, if that is what he wants, we can co-parent. Unlike me, he certainly has the money to fly back and forth, so it shouldn't be a problem.

Everything will be fine, I tell myself, as I dodge Maria's questions and go back out to the car.

When I get back into the car, though, Grayson isn't looking at me. His knuckles have gone white on the steering wheel.

"You took my son," he says in a low voice, and I take in a deep breath. I want to defend myself, to tell him that I did what I thought was best, but he doesn't let me, turning his head to look at me, his bright blue eyes narrow and his gaze is harsh. Cold. "You won't get away with this."

3

GRAYSON

"What do you mean, Grayson?" Lillian asks, biting her lip, looking away from me. I hate it that she won't make eye contact with me. This is exactly what she'd done the day before she left, barely looked at me, barely talked to me.

Usually, I can push down my emotions. I consider it a skill, actually, especially in my line of work when I have to be calm and collected to close the deals that my father needs me to close.

Right now, though, the rage rising up inside me seems endless, unstoppable. I've never hated someone as much as I hate Lillian, and I thought I was over her. I *am* over her, it's just that I didn't expect her to have my child. She hid my child from me. For years. And I'm supposed to just roll over and take it?

"I'll take him," I say, and Lillian gasps, clutching at me. I throw her hand off me immediately, hating the way my heart skips a beat when she touches me. I'm not listening to my heart right now. I'm listening to my head, and my head *hates* her.

"You... you can't do that, Grayson. He's my son."

"He's *my* son!" I roar at her, and she flinches. Five years ago, I would have hated to see her look afraid of me, but now I almost feel vindicated. I'm a formidable enemy, and Lillian would do well to remember that.

"He's *our* son," Lillian says quietly, her voice shaking. "I'm a good mother, Grayson."

"Really? Because I don't remember being informed of having a son, Lillian. And you let him ride the bus?" I scoff, and Lillian takes in a deep breath.

"Cars are expensive, I just—"

"You know I would have gotten you a car," I cut her off. I don't say that I would have gotten her anything, would have done anything, but it's implied. She knows that. She has to know that.

"I didn't think..." she trails off.

"You *didn't* think," I agree. "You didn't think, but now you're going to, because I want my son in my life."

"Look, I'm sorry, okay? I'm sorry I left. I had to. You have to understand." Tears are trailing down her face as she pleads, looking up at me with those big brown eyes. "Please. You can't take him away from me, Grayson, please."

"I think you know that I can," I say coldly, and Lillian begins to actively cry, and I can't look at her. She hasn't lost a single iota of her beauty in the past five years, even after having my son, and it hurts my heart to see her crying. This is why I listen to my head, instead. It's gotten me this far.

"Please, don't," she begs, and I remain silent until she grabs at my shoulder. I shrug her off again, but she doesn't stop looking at me. "Grayson, you can't. He's my baby, I can't lose him. I'll do anything."

I freeze. Having a child out of wedlock would certainly be a scandal for a Whitlock, particularly me, the only son.

The heir. My parents are going to throw a fit, and I know that. There may be something I can do to mitigate things...

Do I really want to do that? Do I want to be around her again, all the time?

Yes, my heart says, but my head tells it to shut up. This isn't about what I feel. This is about what makes sense, what will look best in the media. I hate being portrayed as a womanizer, as someone who just floats through life on my father's money. This will only make that worse.

"Anything?" I ask, and Lillian nods eagerly.

"Anything, Grayson, I swear. Please don't take Max from me,," she says brokenly, and fuck, I can't look at her anymore.

I turn my face away, focusing on the road as I pull out. I plan on just driving, not sure where I am in this town where the snow is still falling. I have no idea what I'm doing, and my heart feels like it's in my throat. I keep telling myself how angry I am, that I'm not hurt, that my heart doesn't ache just looking at her. I'm livid, and I focus on that.

"Then you'll marry me," I command, and Lillian goes silent and still.

"Yes," she says finally, in a broken whisper, and my lips twist in a bitter smile.

There's something so bittersweet about this, about her saying yes to this arrangement instead of actually staying with me. But this is the right thing to do. This way, I get to be with my son (*Max*, I remind myself. *Your son's name is Max*), and Max won't be deprived of his mother. I can keep tabs on her this time, too, make sure that she doesn't abandon our son the way she abandoned me.

"Can I trust you?" I ask her, knowing that I can't, knowing that I never will.

"When it comes to Max, I'll do anything you say," she

says quietly, and I look over at her. She looks defeated, her shoulders slumped, and part of me feels victorious, but most of me hates what I have to resort to, even if for a moment I get to make her feel the way she made me feel all those years ago.

She took something from me, took all the moments of my son's life that I should have been there for, and it's perfectly normal to hate her for that. I don't hate her anymore for what she did to me, but this? This is a whole other reason to reignite my anger and feelings of resentment. If she thinks this is going to be a walk in the park, she has another thing coming.

"We need to set ground rules," I say, and Lillian blinks. I keep my eyes on the road, but I can see her shift in the seat in my peripheral vision.

"Rules?"

She sounds so small, so uncertain.

I clear my throat. "For all intents and purposes, this will be a marriage of convenience. You'll have your own room, your own spending money," I state, and she nods slowly.

"That sounds fine," she says woodenly, but I continue.

"The press needs to think we're together and happy, and so do my parents."

Lillian winces at the mention of my parents, although I can't imagine why. She's never even gotten to meet them, after all. I had wanted her to. I had wanted so many things, but I can't think about that now. Right now, all I need to think about is how to make this work. I need to be thinking about my son, and my son only.

"That makes sense," she says, sounding like she's far away, like she's barely paying attention.

Maybe she's not. Maybe she's so worried about me

taking our son away that she can't think, but I don't care. She needs to hear this.

"You won't see anyone else," I say, and that part sounds firmer than I mean it to. "I don't know what you have going on here, but we'll be flying home and you can't take your boyfriend with you."

I don't tell her that the same rule applies to me, because she probably doesn't care. In the event that she *does*, I don't mind making her sweat and worry about me seeing someone else.

I sound bitter, but why wouldn't I? She deprived me of five years of my son's life. She *left* me and took our child with her. I'll be damned if I let her carry on an affair while I'm trying to make things work for our son and for my reputation. She's the one that ruined everything, so she's the one that's going to have to fix it.

"That won't be a problem."

I can't help the relief that flows through me at that, but of course, I've always been possessive. Not necessarily of the flings that I'd been through before Lillian, but definitely when it comes to her, and I guess that doesn't just go away with time. It's just my territorial nature, and it's normal to be a bit jealous of your ex with someone else, right? In any case, I'm glad that I don't have to worry about another man getting in between myself and my son.

Max is the only thing that matters to me right now. Lillian's comfort, my own comfort—that goes right out the window when it comes to my son. He'll be happier in a two-parent household, and that's all that matters. As a bonus, my reputation will go up, having a wife and child, and my parents will be happy that I've settled down.

"Family men sell more, Grayson," my father says often,

and although I don't know if I agree with him, I guess we'll see.

"Do you agree to the terms I've set out?" I ask her, businesslike, and Lillian's quiet for a moment.

"I agree," she says, and then puts her hands on the dashboard as if bracing herself. "Let's get married.

4

LILLIAN

I've only been on a plane once before in my life, fleeing California. I didn't know I was pregnant yet, but I had terrible air sickness in coach. Fortunately, we're in first class now, and Max has passed out immediately upon take-off. He's never been on a plane, but he always falls asleep on the bus and in cars, so it makes sense.

Max is sitting between us, the excitement of moving to a new city having worn him out, and his head is in his father's lap. Grayson strokes his hair, looking down at him with such fondness that it makes me want to cry.

Grayson will never look at me like that again, and all the "rules" he's set out for our marriage further cemented that. What am I even *doing*? I'm marrying a man that I fled from five years ago, a man that I abandoned without a word. The man I loved. Still do. He didn't love me back then. And as things are, he never will.

I'm biting my lip to shreds when Grayson puts his hand on my knee. When I look up, he's frowning at me.

"Stop that. You'll make yourself bleed." He takes a

napkin and presses it against my lips, and my heart is pounding out of my chest at the simplest touch.

Does he know what he still does to me? Does he know that my heart nearly jumps into my throat every time he looks at me? He can't. And even if he does know, he doesn't care.

Grayson turns away from me, moving his hand to stroke Max's dark hair. I probably could have gotten away with having Max if he didn't look so damn much like his father, but he does.

It's like Max got all of Grayson's genes and barely any of mine, so it's obvious who he belongs to. The second that Grayson had seen him, I felt all the blood drain from my face because I knew that he knew.

Now, I'm going to be stuck in a loveless marriage. No, even worse. A marriage in which my husband can't stand the sight of me. I sigh heavily but Grayson ignores me, still looking down at Max. I feel a pang of sympathy for him. He's missed so much of Max's life–his first steps, his first words, his first day at pre-school. It isn't surprising that Grayson hates me for it, but I can't say that it doesn't hurt, nonetheless.

I brought all I could carry in the little time we had to go to the apartment. I had to beg to go there to get the mementos of our lives, photo albums, Max's favorite toys, and a few changes of clothes for the both of us.

If or when Grayson wants to, I'll gladly tell him all about Max's life and show him all his victories and a few of his misfortunes. The choice I made years ago was made out of survival instinct, but now that he knows everything, I want him to be able to have access to the little frozen memories of Max as a baby and a toddler.

He told me in no uncertain terms that this will be

strictly a marriage for show, and as such, we are going to get married at the courthouse with one of his friends as a witness. I don't know any of his friends. In fact, I barely know anyone in California. I cut everyone off when I had to move away, so I don't expect to have many friends out here.

I have to do this, though. Otherwise, Grayson will take my son from me, and it won't be hard for him to do so. I don't have money for fancy lawyers. I'm barely living paycheck to paycheck as it is. Grayson has both money and status.

I don't want his money. Never did. And I find myself thinking that being his wife can't be that bad, can it? I never forgot him. Never stopped loving him. For the past five years , I have been looking at his face every time I look at my son. And secretly, when I let myself be true to my feelings, I crave his touch, dream about it, about how he slid his mouth down my body, leaving little kisses between my small breasts, stuck his tongue into my bellybutton with his hands down my pants.

Our relationship was a whirlwind. Months of living in this little love bubble, making love and kissing and talking. Months of falling hard in love with the man of my dreams. Months that at the same time felt like seconds, because our time together was so short. But it also felt like decades, because we got to know each other so much. Or so I thought. I gave it my all, and I thought he had too. It was so real for me. Until I learned it wasn't real at all, not for him. So I had to leave. I wanted him to be happy and I wanted to be able to lick my wounds and learn to live a life without him. And then that little plus sign changed my whole reason to live.

I take a deep breath and look over at Grayson once

more, grateful that he has his eyes closed and appears to be asleep. I can look at him to my heart's content, now.

The line of his nose is long, Roman, and his chin and jaw are sharp. He has a dimple in his cheek that only shows up when he smiles, which he never does in my direction anymore. Max makes him laugh, though, and I love to see it.

I'm not surprised that he hates me, but it stings.

Is there a part of me that agreed to this marriage because I feel like he might give in and touch me, make love to me again? Maybe even fall in love with me again?

I can't deny that there's some delusional part of me that thinks that, with time, maybe things will change. It's stupid, and when Grayson opens his eyes, I avert mine, embarrassed and blushing.

Grayson looks at his watch. "We're landing in fifteen minutes," he says, shifting to put Max more in his seat, moving to buckle our son's seatbelt.

I nod, unable to speak. I don't know what I can say. *I wish things were different. I'm sorry.* Those words seem too small, not enough to convince him of what really happened five years ago. I hate the way he looks at me, the way he talks to me, but I'm hoping that once we're married... once we spend some more time together... Maybe I can earn his forgiveness. Maybe he'll understand. I know that the truth will hurt him, and if someone has to hurt, has been hurting all along, that someone is me. And no matter how much he hates me, how badly he treats me, all I ever did was for him. And then for Max. So, I know he is hurting now, but I rather he takes it out on me than be crushed by the real truth of what caused me to leave. I have been hurting for five years, I can hold on for a few more. For Max, I'll do anything. Even take the blame I don't fully deserve.

I sigh as we walk down the runway, with Grayson

holding a sleeping Max. It's stupid to think that way, to think that maybe one day, Grayson will stop hating me. It's a stupid reason to get married, but I need to remember that Grayson has the money and power to take Max from me. I can't allow him to do that. Even if I've wronged Grayson, I've always been a good mother.

When Grayson speaks, his voice is low so as to not wake our son.

"I took the liberty of hiring a babysitter for tonight." He turns to look at me, his mouth twisted in some bitter semblance of a smile. "Since it's to be our wedding night."

I freeze, stumbling over my feet, but Grayson just chuckles. What does he mean by that? Does he want something more from me? Something like... wifely duties?

Would it really be so bad, though? Making love to him again? I don't think it would be, but it would certainly be different. I won't see the love in his eyes anymore, won't feel it in his touch. It'll be something wrong and broken, but if it's all I can get...

"Our wedding night," I repeat under my breath, and Grayson keeps walking as if he hasn't heard me.

THE COURTHOUSE in Los Angeles isn't exactly where I'd imagined getting married, and it's packed, names being called rapidly. It's a lot busier here than it is in upstate New York, that's for sure.

Grayson's jaw is clenched as he looks around, tapping his foot impatiently.

"What's wrong?" I ask, and he doesn't even look at me.

"The stupid witness is late," he growls, looking down at his watch. "If we don't have a witness, we can't get married."

Something oddly logical and rational washes over me, and I think that now is the time that I tell him this is a bad idea. He hates me, I barely know him anymore. We can't get *married*. Surely, he'll come to his senses when I explain, and even though it might ruin my chances of ever touching him again, we'll both be happier and so will Max. Right?

I open my mouth to protest, but a handsome if disheveled man, a bit younger than Grayson going by his boyish good-looks, comes running up to us.

"Lox, thank God," Grayson groans. "I didn't think you'd make it."

"I wouldn't miss my best friend's wedding for the world," the man, Lox, presumably, drawls. I smile a little as he winks at me.

Grayson looks over at me, frowning, and takes my hand in a tight grip, pulling me toward the window as they call, "Whitlock, Grayson."

He shoves all the paperwork toward the open window, and the girl behind it pops her gum, looking up at him like she'd rather be anywhere else. I can understand that, especially since my stomach has started doing flips.

I can't do this. What am I doing? There's no way they'll let us get married this way, right? Is signing paperwork and doing a simple blood test all it takes? Shouldn't someone be *monitoring* this? I'm beginning to panic, my throat feeling tight, but Grayson's grip on my hand doesn't loosen.

"Congratulations," the girl behind the counter says dryly. "Please wait in the next room for the final ceremony."

Final ceremony? So, this isn't a done deal, then? I'm not married.

Keep it together, I tell myself. *He won't go through with it. He can't stand you.*

It stings, but it's true. I don't have to worry because Grayson will never actually go through with it. I'm sure of it.

I barely remember standing up, Grayson's hand still punishingly tight around my fingers, barely listening to what the man standing in front of us is saying.

"I now pronounce you man and wife," he says. "You may kiss the bride."

Grayson leans down, barely brushing his lips against the corner of my mouth, but his best friend, Lox, starts to whoop and holler.

"Yeah! Way to go!" he cheers, and I can't help laughing. It's all so ridiculous, after all.

Grayson frowns and doesn't even say goodbye to his friend, taking me out the back to the parking garage where he parked.

I tug my hand out of his, huffing out a breath.

"Fuck," I curse. "We just got *married*," I mumble under my breath.

Grayson stops in his tracks.

"It's a bit late to have cold feet, Lillian," he says coldly.

Lillian. Never *Lil,* or *baby* like it always had been before. Before my reality check happened. Before I ruined everything.

"I don't have cold feet," I insist, and Grayson snorts out a laugh.

"Didn't seem like it, the way you were laughing at everything that idiot Lox did."

I catch up to him and he rubs a hand across the back of his neck, continuing to walk toward the car.

"Isn't that 'idiot' your best friend?" I ask curiously, and Grayson shrugs.

"I guess. Is he your type? Big and loud, never taking

anything seriously? Is that why..." he trails off, and I frown, putting my hand on his shoulder.

"Is that why what?" I ask softly, hoping that he'll open up just a little, but something so brief I can't recognize flashes across his face before his features shutter up again.

"Nothing." He pulls out of my grasp and opens the door for me. "Your chariot awaits, Mrs. Whitlock," he says, but there's something so bitter about it that I can't even smile.

5

GRAYSON

Back at my house, Lillian walks around as if she's in a dream, going from room to room. I lead her to the guest room, which is half the size of the master bedroom. It's still nice, but not nearly as nice as my bedroom. I suppose part of me wants to punish her, but it's not easy to do that when I live in a mansion.

"This will be your room," I say, swinging the door open, and Lillian looks around in awe. She doesn't speak.

In fact, she's barely spoken since all this began, since I saw her with my son in upstate New York. She's giving in to everything a little too easily, and it makes me want to push her.

I walk into her room as she looks around and I advance on her, backing her up against the wall. She swallows hard, looking up at me with big brown eyes.

"Grayson," she whispers, and suddenly a flash of memory spikes through me like a knife. I remember her saying my name, like a prayer on her lips, how she'd almost breathed it when she was arching under me.

I lick my lips, trying to rid myself of the memory even as it makes me plump in my slacks.

"What's wrong, Lillian? Are you afraid I'll ask you to perform your wifely duties?" I can't help the way one corner of my mouth turns up as she blushes.

"You wouldn't," she insists, but the way she's clenching her fists next to her lets me know she doesn't truly believe that.

"I would never force you to do anything you don't want to do," I insist, even though I don't move away. "You should know me better than that."

"Should I?" she asks, and I want to yell, want to slam my fists on either side of her.

Of *course,* she should know that. Of course, she should know me, but I guess that she never felt the same way about me as I felt about her, or she would know that.

"You don't know me at all, do you?" I find myself asking, cursing myself inwardly. I don't want her to have any idea how much she hurt me back then.

Lillian continues looking up at me, her hands loosening from fists to move to my chest, clutching at my lapels.

"What if I did?"

I frown. "What if you did what?"

"What if I did know you? What if... what if I wanted to?" she whispers, and I blink down at her, my mind screaming at me to back away, to tell her to get away from me, to not let myself get pulled back into her web.

But fuck, she is so beautiful. She's still so sexy to me, even though before her, I'd never dated anyone who looked like her. I'd told myself over and over she wasn't my type as I started to fall in love with her. I'd been stupid then, and I'm stupid now for even considering it.

"It wouldn't be like before," I warn, my eyes searching her face, and she turns her little chin up, as if in defiance.

"I know that."

"Do you?" I ask softly, moving my hand to trace my thumb across her cheekbone, down the line of her jaw.

I shouldn't have touched her, because I feel a zing through my fingertips, almost as if she's burned me, but god. It's like her skin calls to me. *She* calls to me like a siren. Lillian is as dangerous as fire, that's for sure, and I just can't help myself from putting my fingers in the flame.

"I can take whatever you've got," she says, a rasp in her voice from exhaustion from the trip or lust, I can't tell, but either way, it's like a dam bursts inside me.

I lean down to cover her mouth with my own, hard and hungry, forcing my tongue into her mouth. She tastes like mint and wildflower honey, the kind she used to put in her tea in the mornings. It's familiar but bittersweet that I recognize the flavor after all these years. I can't stop, diving my tongue deeper into her mouth. My hand squeezes her jaw between my fingers to open her mouth and she moans against my lips, her body melting into me, her hands on my chest going limp. She's like a ragdoll under my fingers, just like she was before, but this time, I'm not going to treat her with such reverence.

I throw her on the bed, roughly, not caring that she bounces twice before I cover her body with my own. I can't stop thinking about how she'd covered her mouth, laughed at Lox's antics. I'm not that kind of guy. I'm not loud and boisterous, and I keep to myself most of the time. Is Lox the kind of guy she wants? Is that why she left?

There are a million questions swirling around my head but instead of letting any of them out, I press my mouth to hers, so tight that our teeth gnash for a second before she opens her mouth, lets me suck on her tongue. This is nothing like the last time we made love. This isn't going to be making love at all, if I have anything to say about it.

I don't love her anymore. I don't. If I keep telling myself that, maybe it'll finally ring true.

Her body still feels the same beneath my hands, except maybe for a slight widening around her hips and ass. It's far from unattractive, and it only makes me harder inside my slacks. I rut against her thigh as she gasps into my mouth, her arms going around my neck, fingers threading through the hair at the nape of my neck. I need a haircut, but she doesn't seem to care.

"Tell me you want me," I command, and she gasps in a sharp breath as I pull away, looking up into my eyes.

She has to say it. I need to hear it, even if this doesn't go any further. I have no idea why she left, other than the fact that she was hiding her pregnancy. I look down at her, wondering if someone else has been kissing that full mouth for the past five years. Anger rises up in me and I can hear my heartbeat in my ears.

"Say it!" I growl.

"I want you. Grayson, please," she pleads, and I know exactly what she's pleading for. She wants me inside her, wants me to fill her up, but I don't know if I can do it.

I hate this. I hate this feeling of wanting her so much when I feel so angry and resentful. I don't know if I *should* do it, despite my body aching to do exactly what she wants. It's my head that's making more sense, knowing that if I breathe her in, I might not be able to exhale her. I might get stuck, just like I was before, and I can't imagine living that kind of life, not with her living in the house with me.

"Fuck," I mutter, my head spinning as if I drank too much, even though I've given up drinking two years ago, after falling into the bottle hard after she left. She's ruined so many things, and I can't let her do it again.

I pull away, looking down at her, how her legs are spread, how her full mouth is open, and I want her. But I don't need her. She's nothing but trouble, and we've been married only a couple of hours.

I'm stronger than this.

"Have a good night, Mrs. Whitlock," I manage, breathing hard, and turn around and exit the room while she frowns at me.

In the shower, when I wrap my fingers around myself, Lillian is all I can think about. Her mouth against mine, the way her skin felt warm beneath my hands. She tastes and smells just like I remember, just like the memories I've been touching myself to for five years. It's pathetic. *I'm* pathetic, but it's the only thing that gets me there.

Now, it's like I come in an explosion, harder than I think I have in years, because in all this time, I haven't allowed myself to touch anyone else. I can't risk falling the way I fell for her, can't risk being hurt like that again. I have a career to build, things to do—and now everything's turned topsy-turvy all over again.

She had my child, my son, and now I have to see her in my house every single day.

What the hell was I thinking, offering marriage?

Breathing hard, I shove the shower curtain back and grab a towel, being too harsh with the way I dry off my skin. The water had been too hot, and it's left red marks on my body where I've scrubbed.

I foresee a lot more of these long showers with Lillian living in my house.

6

———

LILLIAN

I can't believe this just happened. What was I thinking? I lie here on the bed for a ridiculously long time, watching the closed door, wondering if he is coming back. Fighting with myself, convincing my heart I don't want him back, but knowing I'm waiting for the door to open, until I hear a shower running. And running. And running.

I idly hope that he's taking a cold shower, because I'm burning, my body hot from his touch. How the hell am I going to do this? I'm supposed to live in this big house right next to Grayson Whitlock and not want him?

Why had he teased me that way? I'd already settled for the fact that this would be a loveless marriage in more ways than one, and I'm embarrassed that my body reacted so quickly to him. I'd been ready to risk it all after just a couple of kisses, a few touches of his hands on my skin.

I've always been an idiot for Grayson Whitlock, and I guess nothing has changed in the past five years, despite how much I thought I had grown.

I huff out a breath and get up, heading to the bathroom. I want a cold shower myself, but I also don't want to give him the satisfaction of knowing that I'm affected. Instead, I change into a big, ratty T-shirt, my comfort pajamas.

The only way that I'm going to get through this first week is with comfort, so I pull out a romance book I'd picked up at the airport. Grayson had raised an eyebrow at my book choices but I'd ignored him.

He seems so *angry*. And though I can understand it, after all I've hidden Max from him for so long, somehow this seems like overkill. For the few months we were together, he never once gave me any indication that he wanted more than a casual fling. Guys like Grayson don't go for girls like me long-term. They just wine and dine us, and then toss us aside.

The only reason he married me now is for appearance's sake, and he's made that abundantly clear, especially now. His body might want me, but the rest of him seems to hate me, and I can understand the visceral rage he seems to have for me. But it still hurts. I know he is mad about Max, but I hadn't known about him when I left. Or maybe he's also mad that I left first, before I gave him the chance to dump me. I thought he'd be grateful that he didn't have to do it. Maybe he needed to be the one to end things. To dump instead of being dumped. Not that I'd dumped him. I couldn't. I wouldn't. But when I realized I had to let him go, I did the only thing I could, I fled as far and as fast as I could. Even if my heart stayed behind.

I let out a long breath as I wriggle down into the covers, my neglected body wanting more attention. I don't allow my hands to trail down, though, can't do that without thinking of Grayson and I don't want to do that right now. I don't want to give in, even if he'll never know.

We had seen Max as soon as we got back to the house. We left him with the babysitter because this wedding was not a happy affair and we didn't want him to witness that. Right now, Max is fast asleep in his room, the babysitter is spending the night to watch over him. So, I'm stuck with a problem that most single mothers have when their kid is unavailable o be a distraction–I don't know what to do with myself.

I remember having free time and having a lot of fun with it, but now that I'm a mother I can't seem to remember what I'd done with all that time. I look at my watch and it's just nearing eight, which means it'll be eleven back in New York.

Thank God my best friend is a lifetime New Yorker and a night owl like me.

"Lil? Where the hell have you been? Did you get kidnapped?" Maria answers, and I bark out a laugh.

"Something like that," I mutter. "I got married."

There's silence on the other line for a long moment.

"You... you did *what*?" Maria screeches, and I wince and hold the phone away from my ear slightly.

"It's a long story, but suffice it to say you'll have to come visit me in Los Angeles."

"*Los Angeles*? What the hell is going on, Lillian Elizabeth Brooks? You better tell me right now," Maria demands, and I sigh heavily. I should have known that she would demand to know what's happening. Maria and I became friends when I moved to upstate New York, and shortly after that, I found out I was pregnant with Max, and she hadn't asked a lot of questions. "Does this have to do with Max's dad? You never did tell me who he was."

"His name is Grayson Whitlock," I tell her, and there's another looming pause on the other end of the line.

"Not *Whitlock*. Not *those* Whitlocks," she whispers, and I nod before realizing she can't see me.

"Yep," I say simply, and I can just imagine Maria's mouth gaping open, her green eyes wide.

"You had a baby with a *billionaire* and you never told me?"

"I'm sorry!" I apologize, laughing softly at her dramatics. "I couldn't."

"Wait, and now you're telling me you're married to said billionaire?" she asks incredulously.

"I am," I confirm, because even if it is just a formality to keep appearances, it is true, and there's a string of screeched curses on the other line.

"What the *hell*, Lillian?"

"I can barely believe it myself," I say dryly. "But don't get excited, it's just temporary."

Is it? Temporary? I guess it has to be. Grayson won't stay settled down and married with someone like me forever. I just have to figure out a way out of this that keeps Max happy and my custody of him intact. I know that Grayson wants to boost his reputation, so I just have to stay in this for a few years, and surely he'll grant me a divorce.

I'm not what he wants, as much as that pains me, and it's clear that he can't stand me, so why would he choose to stay in a marriage with me forever? The thought is sobering and my smile fades.

"You have a lot more explaining to do. When can I come and visit?"

"I'll talk to Grayson," I tell her.

"Your *husband*," she says in wonder.

"My h-husband," I stutter, the words feeling strange in my mouth but my stomach seems to fill with butterflies.

"Jesus Christ," my best friend mutters. "What the hell have you gotten yourself into?"

"I have no idea," I say honestly, and we only chat for a bit more before I tell her that I have to go tend to Max, even though that's a lie. I certainly don't want to tell her what just happened in my bedroom and why I can't talk anymore. I can barely think, after all of that, although my conversation with Maria has cleared my head a little.

I look around the bedroom, at the ornate trim around the ceiling and hardwood floors. How much had this house cost to build? Hundreds of thousands? Millions?

Probably the latter.

When I was young, I used to imagine my wedding. I remember thinking that my husband would be tall, dark, and handsome. That much had panned out. I also remember thinking that he'd love me more than anything, more than my foster parents ever had, more than I loved myself, and that part, I'm missing.

Did he ever love me? I can't say for sure that he did, even though I'd fallen head over heels for him. I never told him how I felt, and he never talked about his feelings. We hadn't talked about much of anything, really, just making out and making love, watching the sun rise in the morning and set at night, in some kind of bubble of lust and... what else?

Was it love?

It had certainly felt like it to me, and I've never felt that way since. I have no idea how he felt back then, but it's clear how he feels now, and it's nothing like I imagined when I was young.

I'd never imagined that on my wedding night, I'd be alone in a big, empty bed with nothing but the faint smell of my husband's cologne.

7

———

GRAYSON

I don't dream, at least not since I was a kid. If I do dream, I don't ever remember it, but this time, it feels so real, so vivid, that I might as well be there in person. The thing is, it isn't so much a dream as it is a memory, and that's much, much worse.

Her smile is wide, her laugh infectious. She hasn't worn clothes in three days, and I'm not complaining. She's nipping at my elbow and bicep.

"What are you doing, petal?" I ask her, laughing, and she makes a face, sticking her tongue out at me.

"Hungry. Need sustenance," she mumbles, and then I realize that my stomach is growling, as well.

"Shit. I guess it has been a while since we ate."

"Women can't live off sex alone," she chirps, and I laugh, loud and open.

God, I love her. I can't wait to tell her, the words are all but bursting out of my throat every time I open my mouth in her presence, but there's a time for everything, my father had told me.

"Bide your time, Grayson," he always said. "There's a time for everything, and bad timing can ruin everything."

The timing with Lillian can't be worse, really, with every-thing going on at my father's company. He's buying out a smaller company, merging all the employees together, and he's warned me to be on my best behavior: no scandals.

I don't see why falling in love has to be a scandal, but I'm a Whitlock, and therefore there are always eyes on me. I've known that since I was very small, and I know that my parents view me as the perfect son first and foremost. If I ever do anything to tarnish that image...

Well, let's just say it won't go over well.

So far, I have been the perfect son, and I think I'm afforded a slip here and there. Not that I consider Lillian a slip, but I know that my parents will. She's a foster kid, doesn't come from money, doesn't have a famous family name. In fact, Brooks is the last name she chose for herself, gotten her name changed at eighteen when she struck out from the Midwest, moving to Los Angeles to make it all on her own.

I admire her so much for that. If I hadn't had my family's help, financially and otherwise, I don't think I would have gotten this far. Lillian is amazing, beautiful inside and out, and tonight, I'm going to tell her that.

I'm going to ask her to be my wife.

Just like that, the comfort and closeness of Lillian's double bed is gone, and I'm standing out in the rain with wilting flowers, ringing the doorbell to her apartment over and over.

"She's not home, you shmuck!" Someone yells, and I take in a deep, shaking breath. I wait for another half an hour before giving up, and when I dial her number, it goes straight to voicemail.

For the next week, I don't shake the bone cold of the rain, and not hearing her voice is like an arrow through my heart, every day.

I jolt awake, sitting straight up in bed, holding my hand

to my chest as if I'm having a heart attack. It aches enough to think so, even though I'm only thirty-three. It's not like I'm in my old age, for God's sake.

I snicker, taking in deep breaths through my nostrils to calm myself. I should tell that joke to Loxton later. He'll get a kick out of it.

I tell myself it has nothing to do with how Lillian merely laughed at his stupid jokes, but if I'm honest with myself, I guess it does. I've always been a tad possessive, but with Lillian? It had driven me nuts when she'd so much as smiled at other men while we were together, and I guess that doesn't go away.

So much doesn't go away, including the hurt I feel while thinking back to that memory, of standing in the rain and ringing that bell repeatedly, waiting for her voice to come through the intercom, for the gate to open. Goddamn it.

I run a hand across my face, stumbling to the bathroom, still half asleep, to wash my face. I look at myself in the mirror and it's nothing like the morning after Lillian left, my eyes aren't bloodshot and my mouth doesn't taste like bourbon and vomit, but it's close enough. I can see the pain way back in my blue eyes and as I brush my teeth, I vow that *she'll* never see it.

When I open the dresser drawer to pull out a pair of socks, I'm haunted by the ring box rattling around in there. It's been rattling around in there for five years, and I guess now it's time to take it out. It's time to give it to her, even though it doesn't mean what it did then.

I don't feel that way about her anymore. I *don't*. No matter how much my heart might want to skip a beat when she looks at me, it's just leftover emotion. It isn't real.

I roll the ring box over in my hand, a sapphire with diamonds around the edges, because she'd told me it was her favorite gemstone. She doesn't deserve it, but otherwise, it will just be taking up space in that drawer, collecting dust. My parents might have raised me with a lot of money, but they hadn't raised me to waste it.

I slide on a pair of slacks and a button-up shirt, having neglected to call my assistant to get my dry-cleaning. Good thing I have taken the week off work, giving my boss (who is also my dad) the excuse that I need to get things done. That much is true, although what I needed to get done would shock them.

Fuck. Seeing this ring, thinking of my parents just reminds me that I have to call them. I have to tell them before some idiot photographer gets a picture of Lillian gardening or something and spreads it all over the news.

Lillian's rifling through the refrigerator when I head into the kitchen, dressed only in a big T-shirt. It looks like a man's T-shirt and my jaw clenches.

"What the hell are you wearing?" I ask, and she jumps, squealing.

She drops a container of kiwi on the ground and the round fruit rolls toward me.

"Jesus, Grayson, you scared the *hell* out of me," she gasps, holding a hand to her chest. I lean down and pick up the kiwi, setting them down on the counter and walking toward her with a frown on my face.

The T-shirt is cinched at the waist, showing off her hips and long legs, but I hate it, hate the idea of another man's clothes touching her body.

"I said, what are you wearing?" I ask in a lower tone, walking toward her, and she swallows hard, looking up at me.

"It's just... just a T-shirt, why? Is there a dress code?"

"Yes," I bark, and she laughs hesitantly.

"You're not joking, are you?"

"I can buy you some appropriate nightwear. Some gowns, something lacy. You should be a lady, not wearing some guy's old, ratty T-shirts," I say firmly, and Lillian looks at me for a long moment.

"I may be your wife, Grayson, but you can't control everything I do."

My jaw clenches even tighter, and I can feel a muscle twitching there.

"You know that's not what I meant."

"Do I? You bring me here, away from my job, away from everyone Max knows, and now you're even telling me what to *wear*?"

"I just don't want Max to think it's okay to walk around in old T-shirts," I try to explain myself, even if it sounds silly to my own ears.

Lillian raises an eyebrow. "Okay. That's a weird parenting hill to die on, but I guess. I have my own nighties, don't buy me anything."

"You didn't bring much luggage," I tell her, and she shrugs.

"I don't need much."

I reach into my back pocket to get my wallet, pulling out a black credit card and handing it to her.

"You'll take this and go shopping, for you *and* Max," I order.

There's the hint of a smile at Lillian's lips.

"But you're not controlling."

"I'm *helping*," I say, exasperated, and she breaks out into a smile that makes me take a step backward, bumping my hip on the kitchen island.

"Thank you, husband," she says, her brown eyes twinkling, and she's *got* to be teasing me, it's the only explanation.

Damnit. I don't know how I'm supposed to do this. This is a monumentally bad idea, marrying Lillian Brooks, keeping her close.

You want her close, something in the back of my head says. *You've wanted her so long.*

I clear my throat, pushing those thoughts away. I want*ed* her, past tense. I don't feel that way anymore.

"You can take the sedan," I instruct her, and she raises an eyebrow again.

"There's more than one car?"

I scoff. "Come on, Lillian. I'm frugal but I'm not cheap."

She bursts out laughing at this, covering her mouth as if surprised at herself, and I hate the way my stomach flips over at the sound.

Just leftover emotion, I tell myself, the complete opposite of that other voice. *You don't feel that way anymore.*

"I need to go out," I say briskly, not bothering to sit down. "Help yourself to anything in the fridge."

Lillian bites her lip. "What about Max?"

"The sitter took him to breakfast. He'll be back by noon," I inform her. I miss the little guy already, how he excitedly tells me about the new cartoons he's watching, his easy smile, the blue eyes sparkling up at me that remind me so much of my own.

"You'll be back before noon?" she asks, looking up at the clock.

It's only seven in the morning, and I don't want to spend more time at my mother's house than I have to, especially given the conversation I'll have to have with her.

"I will," I assure her, and grab a banana from the counter. As I do so, I place the ring box down on the counter. I start peeling the banana as I walk out into the garage. I don't look back.

I take the sports car, a two-seater with a manual transmission. It's among my favorites, even though it might be cliché. It makes me feel powerful in a way that the sedan doesn't, even though I suppose I should look into a minivan now that I have a son to take care of. I might need to take Max and his friends to soccer practice or something.

I don't mind the way my heart swells when I think about Max. Before a few days ago. I didn't even know if I wanted kids. Seeing Max for the first time had been like falling in love at first sight–even more powerful than anything I'd ever felt for his mother, honestly.

Max is my focus now, more than my career, more than making my parents proud. It's strange how the world can tilt on its axis and change everything, but sometimes, it does.

It only took me a little under half an hour of traffic to pull up to my mother's mansion. I call it my mother's in spite of the fact that my father's name is on the deed because he doesn't live there, not anymore. He has his own penthouse apartment in Los Angeles. My parents married for all the right reasons, but none of those reasons included love, and when I went to college, they separated physically if not legally.

Divorce is frowned upon in my Catholic family, and in my parents' eyes, marriage is for status or convenience. I guess it's all the money and the fact that my mother hadn't signed a pre-nuptial agreement. That was the first thing I had Lillian sign, and she'd made no bones about it, fortunately. I want my son in my life, and unfortunately, that means having his mother in my life, too. As much as I resent Lillian for what she did, I want my son to grow up with both parents.

It has nothing to do with me wanting her close, even in some locked away portion of my heart. This is all for Max, just like everything will be now.

My mother doesn't bother coming to the door when I knock, just calling for me to come in. I walk back toward the kitchen, where I know she'll be sitting with her morning glass of white wine, complete with two ice cubes, no more, no less.

"Mother?" I call, and she sighs heavily, looking up at me.

"You only call me Mother when you've done something wrong. What is it, Grayson?"

I sit down across from her, wishing that I had gotten here a bit later, when the glass would be half empty instead of full. Maybe she would take the news better after a second glass.

"I wouldn't exactly call it wrong," I say slowly, and my mother's blue eyes narrow.

"Grayson Theodore Whitlock," she warns, and I put my hands up in defense.

"I've gotten married," I tell her, and I pull out of my phone quickly, showing her pictures of Max that I'd taken at the airport and the brief time we'd spent at home before the wedding. "And this is Max."

"Oh my God," my mother breathes, and I know that just from the sight of him, she knows, just like I had.

I nod. "Max is my son, Mom," I say softly, knowing this is a big bomb to drop, and my mother scrolls through the pictures, her eyes soft for a moment before she looks up at me, her face completely changing.

"What do you mean, you got married? This boy has to be four or five years old, Grayson," she snaps.

I don't back down. I haven't been afraid of my mother since I was ten years old.

"It was... a fling I had, five years ago," I tell her, and slow realization comes over my mother's face. She remembers how I'd gone off the rails five years ago, nearly ruining my reputation by being out drunk in public way too often.

"Grayson," my mother scolds. "You've never been one to chase women."

"It was a mistake," I admit. "But I got something wonderful out of it. Look at him, Mom."

She looks down at the phone in her hand, scrolling through the pictures with one manicured nail.

"He's beautiful," she says softly, and I know that at least with Mom, I've got the okay.

"Thank you." I feel proud somehow, even though all I'd done so far for Max is give him half my DNA. That's going to change.

Then, my mother's face changes, hardening again.

"You will have a wedding," she says firmly, and I frown.

"I'm already married."

"You *will* have a wedding," she repeats, her voice harsh. "The media will want a wedding. Your father will want a wedding. We need to meet this girl, of course."

"Of course," I say, trying not to roll my eyes. I know that will just make things worse. I should have known my mother would be barking orders at me the second I told her.

"You'll bring my grandchild to visit," she insists, but this time her voice cracks just a little, and I smile.

My mother has always been the more sensitive of my parents, and I can tell that she will have a good relationship with Max. My father, on the other hand? I'm not so sure.

"I haven't told Dad yet," I confess, and my mother nods.

"Don't you worry about your father. I'll tell him," she assures me, and pauses before she reaches over and caresses my cheek with her thumb. "You did the right thing coming to me, Grayson."

I take her hand in my own, turning my face into her palm. I love my mother in that moment more than I maybe ever have. My parents have always been standoffish. Affection was rare in our household growing up, but my mother had always seemed to understand me in a way that my father didn't. I'm glad that she seems to understand this situation, as well.

"I should get back to my wife," I tell her, even though there's something ridiculous about that statement, right after my sham of a marriage.

My mother looks up at me curiously. "Do you love her?"

I'd started to stand up, so I pause, looking down at her.

"Does it matter?"

My mother doesn't answer, and I leave the house feeling better than I had when I came in. At least I have her on my side, and she would handle things with my father, at least to begin with.

Now it's time to go back to my wife, hope she's changed out of that old boyfriend's T-shirt, or whatever it is, so that I won't want to rip it off her and throw her over my shoulder like a caveman, take her to my bed (now our marital bed, technically), and show her who she belongs to.

I shake my head, the sudden thoughts making something jealous and vicious raise up in my throat. I can't think that way about her, not anymore. She's the mother of my child, and no matter how much I once wanted her, I can't fall back into those patterns.

It's a marriage of convenience, and even if I plan for it to last forever, I won't let myself fall again. I can't.

8

———

LILLIAN

"Where's Daddy?" Max asks, and I take in a deep breath. I'm still not used to him asking those kinds of questions, even a week after our marriage and move across country.

"He's meeting with your Grandma," I tell him, and Max grins.

"I love Grandma," he says sweetly, and I smile down at him. Grayson has taken Max over to visit with her a couple of days ago, and warned me that I also needed to meet her.

"She's nice," I say dryly, even though I don't really think so, but that's something I don't want to think about right now.

"I like this cake," Max says, poking a finger into the frosting, and I wrinkle my nose.

"Ew, now you've made it all gross," I tease, and Max giggles, popping his finger into his mouth.

I can't believe that I'm picking out a wedding cake from samples, but Grayson's busy with picking the colors of the suits and bridesmaid dresses. I had thought that getting married at the courthouse would be the end of it, but Grayson's mother insists on a "real" wedding.

According to Grayson, the media will even be there, so I have a lot to plan and think about. I don't know if I want to be plastered all over television as Grayson Whitlock's wife. What happens when we get this marriage annulled or get divorced? Grayson surely doesn't intend to keep up this charade forever.

Does he?

I guess that's something I need to ask him about, but it's not like he's very chatty when we're alone together. The most he does is criticize my choice of sleeping clothes. The morning after we'd had that ridiculous argument about me wearing "appropriate" sleepwear, I'd put on a lacy nightie for the next night.

When I was making coffee, he grunted behind me to let me know he was there.

"Don't like this one, either?" I asked, half teasing, and Grayson made another grunting sound in the back of his throat.

"Too short," he said, and I huffed out a long breath, sliding his coffee to him before storming into the guest bedroom I pretty much lived into.

I can't do anything right for Grayson Whitlock, and that's all there is to it. I've been taking it with grace, but lately, I've begun to push back, at least a little. I can't spend my whole life bowing down to what he wants.

"Do I get to stay with Grandma after the wedding?" Max asks, and I frown a little.

Grayson's family has insisted on it, that we have a "honeymoon" for a long weekend, but I can't think of anything I want less.

Grayson barking at me or ignoring me for three nights and four days? No, thanks.

"I think this is the one," I say, smiling at the baker as she comes over to check on us. She gives Max a high five and I realize there's still frosting all over his hand with a wince.

She doesn't seem to care, though, and Max grins as I wipe frosting off his face. He'll be bouncing off the walls from all the activity and sugar, but oh well. The kid deserves to be a kid once in a while. I think for most of his life, I've been working so hard that I haven't been the best mom, and the one thing about this brief marriage is that I can spend more time with him.

Grayson made it clear that he doesn't want me to further my career, wants me to stay home with Max, and that's not something that's going to last forever. There's no way I can just sit at home and be a homemaker for the rest of my life. I also can't be celibate for the rest of my life, especially living with an incredibly attractive man. I guess I have plenty of practice on that front, at least, since I haven't been intimate with anyone since Grayson.

I know it seems a bit pathetic, and I'd been on a few dates and had a couple of goodnight kisses, but for one, I'd been too busy, and for two, no one compares to Grayson.

Shit. I am kind of pathetic.

I focus on Max, loading him into the sedan that Grayson has told me is mine to use as I wish.

"You know what, Mom?" Max says innocently.

"Mmm?" I'm distracted, turning into traffic.

"I think ice cream would be a great end to this day."

"Oh, do you?" I ask, laughing a little. "Okay, I think we can make that happen."

~

Max falls asleep in the car on the way back home after the exciting day full of cake and ice cream, and I'm a little bit grateful. The business of the city and the balmy weather have made me feel a little dirty, and I know that Grayson has a hot tub in the master bathroom. He won't be back for hours, so I can use it while he's gone.

After I put Max down, I undress in my room and streak across to Grayson's bedroom, biting my lip as I stand naked in his room, telling myself not to snoop. It occurs to me suddenly that Grayson might be seeing someone. He might have several someones he's seeing, really. Why would he be faithful to me in this sham of a marriage?

In the end, I just sigh and walk into the bathroom, turning the water on as hot as I can stand it and sliding down into the tub when it's ready, turning on the jets and letting out a long moan as they massage my lower back. I need this after this crazy last couple of weeks, that's for sure.

Grayson set plenty of rules for our marriage, but he never said I couldn't use the hot tub, so although I'm not directly breaking a rule, it feels kind of naughty to be in his space, like I'm really his wife. I can see his razor and after-shave on the sink, a discarded pair of jeans he hasn't quite thrown in the laundry basket.

Grayson isn't all that put together, after all, I think with a smile. He certainly hadn't been so tight-lipped and stuck-up when I'd known him, but I guess that was a long time ago.

I can't help thinking about him back then, how his hair had been longer, his eyes brighter, no frown ever on his face. There had always been a hint of a smile at the corner of his lips. He had touched me almost like I was something holy, his fingertips light on my skin.

I can't help the way my fingers trail down between my breasts, moving to slide my thumbs across my nipples. I gasp and it's not audible over the jets of the hot tub. Max is a heavy sleeper, anyway, but I'm grateful for the background noise as I get louder, sliding my hands down to my lower stomach.

I moan loudly when my thumb slips against my clit, and I clamp my other hand over my mouth to mask the sound.

"He can't hear you, he's fast asleep," a low, husky voice says from the doorway, and I gasp, my eyes popping open to see Grayson standing there, looking down at me with lust-filled blue eyes.

"Grayson, shit, I'm sorry—" I sit up, moving my hands away, and he shakes his head.

"No, naughty girl. Keep going. You snuck in here already. Damage is done."

Oh *shit*. Am I dreaming this? Is Grayson really saying that, standing in front of me?

I pivot in the hot tub to face him, my face feeling hot.

"I'm sorry that I snuck in," I say dumbly, bracing my hands on the sides of the hot tub.

Grayson sits down on the closed toilet, looking at me intently.

"Make it up to me," he says, and I choke on air.

"What do you mean?"

"You know what I mean," he says, his words firm if not harsh, exactly, his tone low.

I swallow hard, thinking. Why am I apologizing, anyway? I'm his wife. This is my house, too, isn't it? I live here with our son; I'm supposed to be a housewife, right? So, why can't I use the hot tub?

"I don't think I've done anything wrong," I say, knowing that I sound like a brat but not caring.

Grayson raises a thick, dark eyebrow. "Is that so?"

"It's my house, too. That's what you said," I remind him.

"Did I say that?" he asked, his mouth turning up at the corner. He looks amused and interested, still staring at my face instead of my exposed breasts.

"You did," I insist, and slowly, watching his eyes flick to my breasts, I cup one in my hand, dragging my thumb across my pebbled nipple.

Grayson licks his lips, his eyes going back to my face.

"Do it again," he orders, and something about the way he asks, firm but also longing, makes me cup my other breast, doing the same on that side and letting out a low moan.

"Like that?" I ask, and Grayson rests his forearms on his thighs, leaning forward, closer to me.

"More," he commands, and I tug at my nipples with my fingertips, my head spinning.

If you had told me when we were at the courthouse that this would be happening just a few days after, I wouldn't have believed you.

I slide my hands down to my stomach again, slipping my thumb against that bundle of nerves and gasp in a breath. It feels so much different with his eyes on me, better, pleasure blooming in my abdomen. I'm glad that I refrained from putting Max's bubble bath into the water, so that he can see everything.

"Spread your legs," he demands, and I do so, bracing them on either side of the tub. My muscles ache, it's been so long since I've been in this position.

Five years, in fact.

"Grayson," I mumble, my lips loose from lust and the heat of the bath making me feel a bit dizzy. I feel almost drunk. "Do you wish it was your fingers?"

"Do you?" he asks, turning it around on me, his eyes hungry on my sex. "I bet my fingers could go deeper."

I slide two fingers up inside my slick heat and cry out. I'm so close to the edge already I don't know if I'll last through all his commands.

"Faster," he tells me, and I listen, arching my fingers up and he's right, his are thicker, would go deeper, get to that place I'm so desperately trying to reach.

I'm on the edge of begging him to get in with me, to finish the job.

"Grayson, Grayson, I'm so close," I plead, but Grayson just keeps looking at the way I'm pumping my fingers in and out, his eyes laser focused, his tongue darting out now and then to wet his lips. He doesn't make a move toward me and I close my eyes as I get close, my mouth popping open in an "o" of pleasure.

"Open your eyes," he barks. "Look at me."

My eyes pop open at the command and I look right into his blue eyes as I come, gasping and rocking my hips against my own fingers.

I'm flushed red all over, now out of embarrassment instead of lust, and I slide my fingers out with a groan.

Grayson stands up and I can see him hard in his slacks, against his right thigh, and I think he's going to cup himself there, take off his pants, let me see, and my eyes are hungry on his crotch.

Instead, he looks at me for another long moment and walks out the door. In just a moment, I hear the car crank up in the garage and I huff out a breath.

What the hell was *that?*

9

GRAYSON

Ever since I embarrassed myself and my family five years ago by dropping the ball after Lillian left, I don't drink. Well, I *do*, but socially, a couple of beers here or there with Lox.

Loxton, on the other hand, drinks like a fish, uncaring about his family's view of him and embracing the playboy reputation the media has given him. So, of course, after seeing Lillian in the hot tub, I call my best friend.

"Hey, Gray, what's good?" he answers, and I want to roll my eyes but I need him for tonight, at least.

"I want to get drunk," I say bluntly, and Lox pauses as if surprised.

"Shit, okay, let's get it!" he cheers. "Meet me at City Walk, would you?"

"Not City Walk," I tell him. "Too many paparazzi. Let's go to that dive bar on the corner."

Lox groans. "Not there, there's never any women. It's always a sausage fest."

"No women is good." I bark out a bitter laugh. "I'm a married man, after all."

"Jesus, I almost forgot about that," Lox says sheepishly, and I wonder if he'd been drunk at the courthouse. I wouldn't put it past him.

I hang up on him and sure enough, he's waiting for me at the bar, a shitty dive literally called "The Dive." They embrace their low-lights, cheap beer, and bad location, and no one would ever think that two billionaires would go there for a night out. It's perfect for what I need tonight.

I order a double bourbon and coke, and Lox raises an eyebrow.

"You really do want to get drunk. What's up with you?" he asks, and I sigh.

I guess there's no harm in telling Lox. He might be an idiot, but he's *my* idiot, and we've been best friends for almost a decade. We grew up in the same circles, although he's quite a bit younger than me, and he's always been like a younger brother. I've always been a lot more put together, but Lox had been the one there for me when everything got turned upside down five years ago.

"I want to fuck my wife," I say bluntly, and Lox spits out his vodka and soda.

"That's a *problem*?" He bursts out laughing. "Isn't that part of the whole deal?"

I shake my head. "Not this marriage," I tell him, and Lox stares at me.

"You married a woman thinking you *wouldn't* want to fuck her? What the hell? She's kind of hot, man—"

"Don't talk about her like that," I growl, and Lox raises his hands as if in defense.

"I'm just stating the facts," he says, but I glare at him anyway. "I know this whole situation is weird, but of course you want to fuck her. She's your ex, right? One of them?"

"The only one," I confess. "I've never had more than a fling before Lillian."

Lox's eyes slowly widen and realization passes over his face.

"Oh, shit. She's *that* girl."

I nod briskly. "Yup."

"Shit," he says again, shaking his head. "So, she's the one you were so fucked up over?"

"She is," I confess, and I can't believe Loxton hadn't already put that together, but he isn't the world's most intuitive person. Lox cares about himself, first and foremost, and booze and women are second and third. I know there's a part of him that isn't that selfish, but not many other people do. Lox doesn't let anyone close, that is, not anyone but me.

"Dude, that's fucked up. Why would you marry someone who hurt you like that? Why not just take her to court?"

"That's a real good question," I say dryly, thinking back. I guess I'd been so gob-smacked by having a son that I didn't know about that I hadn't thought clearly.

Now, I'm stuck with a wife I can't stand but very much desire, and she's in my house every day, tempting me in little nighties or touching herself in my hot tub... Fuck. What am I going to do about it?

"So, get an annulment," Loxton suggests, and I frown. That doesn't seem like a good option to me, and not just because of Max. My parents would hate the media attention that legal documents would invite. And I couldn't keep an eye on Lillian.

Damnit. Is that part of the reason I married her? To keep her close, watch out for her, make sure she isn't seeing anyone else? I have to admit to myself that it is, but it's out of spite more than it is of love.

I don't love her anymore, and that's something I have to

keep reminding myself. And she never loved me at all. That much is clear.

Loxton orders us a couple of tequila shots and I take one gratefully, wincing at the burn as it slides down my throat.

"I can't get an annulment," I say, finally answering his question. "She'll go after custody of Max."

"So? You have the money for lawyers and you're a billionaire. They won't give her custody."

"They side with the mother a lot," I mumble, but that isn't quite it. Lillian is a good mother, and if I annul the marriage, what happens? She leaves, and I'm stuck with Max alone? I don't think that she'd do that. I think she'd be in my life one way or the other if we are married or not, so I might as well keep up the farce.

"So fuck her," Lox says easily, and I stare at him.

"That's not an option."

"Why *not*? It's only been a hundred years since you got laid, and now you're *married*. Ask her to be friends with benefits or whatever."

I snort out a bitter laugh. "Friends with benefits. We were never friends."

"You're still in love with her," Loxton says in awe, ordering us another round of shots. "That's what all this is about. That's why you don't want an annulment."

"I'm not," I say firmly, and if I keep saying it out loud, maybe I'll believe it. My heart still feels empty when I think about Lillian, even when she's living in the bedroom next to mine, and I don't know how to deal with it. The problem is that I am still attracted to her, but it can't be love. Not anymore. Not again.

"What's the plan here, Gray? Are you going to just sit by when she gets a boyfriend? Let her go on dates?"

I slam my glass down on the bar. "Absolutely not. That's one of the house rules."

Lox scoffs. "You have got to be kidding me. You expect her to be celibate like you for God knows how long? You know she's eventually going to meet somebody."

"We need to change the subject," I grumble, feeling possessiveness and jealousy rise in my stomach, making me feel nauseous. I don't want to think about Lillian seeing someone else, especially in my house! I would lose my mind and I know that.

"I'm serious, Gray. You've got to figure out a game plan, here. If you don't want her, you can't stop her from—"

"I *do* want her," I burst out. "I want her so much it's killing me, but I can't let myself... " I trail off, not sure what I mean, or not wanting to say it out loud.

I can't fall back in love with her. It'll kill me.

I can't say that to Lox, who has nothing to compare love to. He's never been in love, never settled down with anyone for more than a couple of months, and he can't understand. Lillian and I had something back then, something real. It's something I still crave, something I want in my life, but it nearly killed me to lose it.

Now, having her close but so far away is nearly killing me too. It's like there's no way to win, so instead of worrying about it, I keep drinking.

Lox's advice is to sleep with her, and as I get progressively more drunk, I wonder if maybe he's right. I could get it out of my system that way. I could do it once and then never again, couldn't I?

Time starts to slip, and the next thing I know, they're calling last call and Lox has his arm slung around my shoulder.

"Now I'm gonna put you in a car and you're going to go

home and fuck your wife," he slurs, and I laugh at the absurdity of the situation.

I don't remember Lox putting me in the car or the trip home, but putting in the alarm code at the door is vivid because the numbers on the pad are blurring and it takes me three tries.

The last thing I remember before I wake up with my mouth feeling like cotton and tasting like death is standing at Lillian's door, leaning against the doorjamb for support.

Lillian is snoring next to me and I blink at her. What the hell did I do last night?

10

LILLIAN

I wake up to the shrill sound of the alarm going off once when Grayson comes into the house. I think I should get up and check on Max, but when I don't hear cries from his room, I know he's slept through it. I roll over and try to go back to sleep myself. I was up late wondering what the hell that scene in the bathroom had been all about.

I can hear Grayson in the house but I assume he's going straight to bed since it has to be late, probably the wee hours of the morning. I haven't looked at my phone but I know I've been asleep a few hours. I yawn and close my eyes.

"Lillian?" Grayson's voice is slurred just around the edges and I know he's been drinking. I sit up, blinking sleep out of my eyes.

"Grayson?" I respond, and he comes toward me in a careen and I can't help but laugh a little when he puts both hands down on the bed to steady himself.

"Are you awake?" he asks belatedly, and I cover my mouth to stop another laugh.

"I am now," I say dryly, and Grayson sits down heavily

on the bed, looking at me with glassy, bloodshot blue eyes that are still beautiful.

"Wanted to talk to you," he mumbles, reaching out to wrap his fingers around my bare ankle. I gasp at his touch, not expecting it.

"Is something wrong?" I ask, and Grayson shakes his head and then nods, and I stare at him, confused.

"Want you," he murmurs low in the back of his throat, the words almost raspy with alcohol and lack of sleep.

A zing of pleasure and anticipation shoots through my body, but I bite my lip, seeing what shape he's in.

"Want me how?"

"The way a husband wants his wife," Grayson says gruffly, and he moves his hand up to my bare knee. I'm wearing one of the nightgowns he spurred me to buy, and his fingers touch just the edge of the lace on my thigh before I draw in a sharp breath.

"Grayson, you're drunk," I accuse, and he nods solemnly.

"I am," he agrees, and instead of moving his hands higher like I expect, he crawls up next to me on the bed, smelling of some acrid liquor and a light scent of sandalwood from the aftershave he uses. He used the same brand when we were together, and I don't think I could ever forget the way it smells.

He's unbuttoned his shirt almost all the way but left it on, and there's an expanse of tanned, muscular chest that I'm finding a hard time keeping my eyes off of.

He fumbles with the covers and I scoot over to let him settle in, but he makes a displeased noise in the back of his throat. He puts his arms around me, pulls me close, buries his face in my neck and inhales.

"Grayson," I say, not knowing what to do, if I should stop

him from making what he'd surely think of as a mistake or if I should give in even if he might not remember it.

"Hmm?" he hums, his lips vibrating against my neck, and then he kisses me there, open-mouthed, nuzzling into me without any urgency, like he's breathing me in.

"What are you doing?" I ask softly.

"Sleeping," he mumbles, and squeezes me tighter until I nearly squeak.

"Um," I manage, but it's no use, his breath is coming slow and even, lightly snoring but his arms stay tight around me.

I tug at him experimentally to see if I can slide out from his arms but he grumbles something in his sleep and just holds me tighter.

I'm trapped. Trapped in the arms of my ex, the only man I've ever loved, the father of my child, and my current husband. In other circumstances, I might have been happy, but I know that Grayson would never have held me like this sober.

"Grayson," I try, but he doesn't respond.

I guess I'm going to have a later night than I thought.

AT SOME POINT, I must have fallen asleep because it's Grayson's hoarse voice that wakes me.

"What the fuck?"

Good question, really. I don't really know how to react and consider pretending to still be asleep, but I figure I might as well have a little fun with this if he really doesn't remember.

"Don't you remember, honey?" I coo, putting my hand on his chest and sliding my fingers across his skin.

Grayson swallows hard. "Fuck. We didn't."

"Didn't what?" I ask, blinking innocently, and Grayson makes a sound between a grunt and a growl and sits up, holding a hand to his head.

"You've got to be fucking kidding me."

I can't help it; I let out a peal of laughter.

"I am kidding you. You just crawled into bed and went to sleep. Have a bad night?"

"You could say that." He rubs a hand across his neck, and I have this urge to touch him.

I reach out to put my hand on his back and he leans into my touch before he stiffens, standing up and looking down at himself.

"You're sure nothing happened?" he asks, and I nod.

"Not since the bathroom," I whisper, and he stiffens again, his shoulders going square.

He doesn't look back at me, just striding out of the bedroom and closing the door behind him.

In a few moments, I hear Max giggling and I assume that Grayson's gone into his room. I roll over on my side, sighing. I'm exhausted. It was hard to fall asleep with Grayson's arms around me. It'd been so long since I'd been held like that...

Before I know it, I'm cuddling the pillow that still smells like him and falling asleep.

When I awake, it's because Max is bouncing on my bed.

"Mommy, mommy, mommy!" he cries. "Daddy's going to take me to the trampoline park!"

I yawn, turning over to pull him on top of me and kissing him all over his face while he groans and yells.

I smile. "I hope you have fun, buddy."

"You're going with us," Grayson says from the doorway, his voice still raspy from the late night.

I sit up, holding Max in my lap. "I am?'

"We're a family, aren't we?" Grayson says gruffly, and I realize he's showered and dressed. His dark hair is damp and he's wearing a black T-shirt and jeans, more casual than he'd been dressed yesterday.

I can't help myself from imagining what he did last night, and with whom. Maybe he'd been out with a girl, on a date or something. It's none of my business, but still, it stings.

Especially since I have to obey his *rules*.

I wonder how long that will go on—until Max is a little older? Until we eventually dissolve this marriage? Until Grayson meets someone else? It makes me feel nauseous to think about that.

Max bounces off the bed and follows his father. I smile fondly after them. He's been Grayson's shadow ever since we came here, and I can't believe he took to him so quickly. I guess that even though I'd kept him from Grayson, there's still a bond there. They share the same blood.

I dress myself quickly in a sundress that's just a little too tight across the hips since I've had Max, but honestly, I haven't bought new clothes in years, except for the nightgowns that Grayson suggested.

I look at myself in the mirror, shrugging and putting on a little light makeup before heading out into the living room.

Grayson throws Max up in the air, over and over, while Max giggles uncontrollably.

"That's what the trampolines will be like," he tells him, and Max's blue eyes widen before he hugs him tightly.

I can see Grayson's normally stoic face change, softening the lines on his face and making him look younger. He kisses Max's cheek and carries him out to the car, not even acknowledging me. I'm not surprised, but I'm still disappointed, sighing as I slide into the passenger seat.

Grayson's busy buckling Max in, and other than Max's occasional questions, the way he sings along to the Disney playlist in the car is the only sound while we drive to the park.

I look over at Grayson, how good he looks in a tight black shirt and jeans, and avert my eyes when he glances at me. I guess this will be an exercise in "keeping up appearances" since we have to have a real wedding soon.

"Any news on a date for the wedding?" I ask, and Grayson clears his throat.

"Saturday."

My eyes widen and I stare at him.

"*Saturday*? When were you going to tell me?"

"I'm telling you now," Grayson barks. "You've picked out a dress, we've got the cake and the venue, what else do you need?"

A loving husband, I think. *Someone who won't just order me to touch myself but will touch and kiss me, make love to me.*

I close my mouth, going silent. It's crystal clear that I have no say in this marriage, and instead of arguing while Max is with us, I'm just going to keep my big mouth shut.

Max runs for the biggest trampoline, tugging Grayson with him. I'm sure that Grayson won't jump with him, but as I watch, he starts to take off his shoes. I just stare at him, surprised. Grayson is a good father, but I never expected him to play with Max as much as he does—especially not in public.

Grayson is a little buttoned-up to be jumping on a trampoline with our son, but apparently, he doesn't care.

Grayson looks at me as I just stand there and he takes hold of my hand, not looking at me.

"Come with us," he says, and it's not really an invitation so much as a command, so I slip off my shoes and slide onto the trampoline in my no-show socks, slipping and almost falling.

Grayson grabs me by the waist to steady me, and I bump against his chest, looking up into those dark blue eyes.

"Careful," he murmurs, looking away from me, and Max is already running full-tilt around the large trampoline, bouncing on his heels, so I ignore the way my heart races and run after my son.

Max giggles and runs faster, but his legs are short and I manage to tackle him. We bounce as we hit the ground, and then Grayson calls out Max's name.

"Watch this," he says with a grin that's just for Max, and I just recline on the trampoline, watching. Max's eyes widen as Grayson jumps and flips over once, landing gracefully.

"Wow!" Max yells. "Show me how?"

Max disentangles himself from me and runs toward Grayson, who laughs when Max tries to flip and fails, falling flat on his face.

Max isn't hurt, and he's more determined than ever to be like his father, so Grayson takes him by the waist and flips him with his hands.

"That's fun, but I wanna do it myself," Max grumbles.

I'm still just lying on the trampoline, watching them, and I smile, thinking of how stubborn they both are. Grayson is athletically built, his shoulders wide and his waist trim, and Max is going to be built the same way. I can tell already that his shoulders are widening as he gets older but he stays thin.

I can't believe I've gone all this time worried about Grayson finding out when Max loves him so much, but on the other hand, the reasons behind me leaving weren't exactly my pregnancy. I hadn't even known at the time.

I'd had my reasons. Valid reasons. And there had been a lot at stake.

I stand up, not wanting to go down that rabbit hole, and almost immediately fall back down because Grayson and Max are bouncing on the trampoline and it propels me forward.

Max laughs at me and tries to help me up, but in the chaos, he falls over too, and Grayson laughs loud and open.

It's a lovely sound, and I look up at him, smiling. He looks down at us for a long moment, something flashing across his face so quickly I can't identify it, and then looks away.

"I think I need a break. I'll be back in a bit," he mutters, and Max hums, uncaring and having a great time, jumping all around me.

I watch after Grayson with a frown, wondering what's wrong. I suppose he's probably hungover, so maybe he's just going to get some water.

But honestly, do I ever know what's going on with Grayson? It's not like he confides in me. I want today to be good, for us to be a family, but it's very clear that it's all for show.

11

GRAYSON

Lillian is driving me crazy in that tight little dress, the way it spreads across her ass showing every curve. Max loves her so much, laughing and playing with her, and it's like an arrow through my heart every time I see them together. It's bittersweet, thinking of all the time I lost, of everything that Lillian took away from me.

It makes me angry, and I can't believe that I still want her so much, that something inside me still longs for her. What is wrong with me?

After everything she'd done, I still can't keep from feeling a particular way when I see a flash of thigh while she jumps. She has to know what she's doing. I wonder if she's punishing me for last night, for crawling into bed with her, falling-down drunk.

It's embarrassing, that I let myself get so out of control, how I wanted her so much I actually went to her room. I blame Loxton entirely, especially since he was the one who'd kept harping that I take advantage of my "marital duties."

Loxton's an idiot, but I guess I forgive him since he's

right - I *do* want Lillian. I want her just as much as I ever had. It's like nothing has changed since the last time that I saw her, and that's dangerous now that we're living in such close quarters.

I had hated seeing her in some guy's T-shirt but the little gowns with lace she bought might be even worse, and now she's wearing a sundress that's *way* too small across her ass. As she jumps with Max, I watch her and see another guy with a kid with his eyes all but bulging out like a wolf in one of those old cartoons.

I shoot him a death glare and he looks away quickly. Damn right. Lillian may be my wife in name only, but I'll be damned if I let anyone else look at her like that. I know it's dangerous to still think of her as mine, but I can't help feeling that way. I can't believe we're having *another* wedding at the end of the week. It's like some kind of specific torture just for me.

I glance back over at Lillian and she's giggling with Max, jumping with him, the dress riding up on her thick thighs. It's hard to watch her with him. She's so good with him, and he loves her so much. No matter how much I hate her, I know now that I could never take Max away from her. He'd be miserable, and I don't want that for my son.

I didn't have love and affection from my mother growing up, and I wouldn't want him to ever have to be without it, which puts me in quite a pickle when it comes to Lillian Brooks-Whitlock. Not to mention that I crawled into her bed last night.

Nothing happened, I would remember it, wouldn't I? She said that I had just gone to sleep, and I think that's pretty close to what happened. I was pretty out of it, after all, after Lox kept buying me shots. I'm nursing one hell of a hangover today, and I don't think I'll be partaking in much champagne at our wedding this weekend, despite how much I love the way it tastes.

Max eventually starts tiring out and getting whiny, clinging to his mother and getting upset when he can't figure out how to flip. I pick him up and he immediately puts his arms around my neck, resting his little head on my shoulder.

My heart feels so full I can't stand it. I've never felt this kind of feeling, like I'd do any and everything for this one little boy. I'd thought, all those years ago, that the only way I'd ever feel this kind of love was for one woman, but the love I have for my son is an entirely different animal: ferocious in its way. If anyone ever tried to take him from me, I'd burn the world down, and so I can understand why Lillian offered to marry me so quickly.

It had nothing at all to do with me, and everything to do with Max, and honestly, I respect that to some degree. She loves our son, and since I can't have exactly what I want, I have to make that close enough.

I clear my throat as we walk out of the trampoline park, and Lillian looks over at me.

"You hungry?" I ask, and she stares at me for a long moment, as if surprised.

"Starving," she admits, and I nod and take Max the rest of the way to the car, buckling him in tight and kissing his temple.

"About last night," I start when I pull the car out onto the interstate.

"Last night doesn't matter," Lillian says firmly. "It's fine."

I don't know what else to do but accept it, nodding slightly and pulling into a nearby barbeque restaurant. I figure that Max will eat some chicken fingers and fries, and it's between the trampoline park and the house, so that he can get a little nap in.

Lillian's quiet, leaning her head against the window, and I want to ask her what's wrong, but it doesn't matter. I need to stop worrying about her, about what she thinks and feels, because none of that matters as long as she's good to Max.

I just have to get through this stupid wedding, and then we can go on living our separate lives in our separate rooms. Lox is wrong—I can do this without sleeping with her. It's just been a long time since I've seen her, and old feelings are coming up, that's all. I'll settle into a rhythm soon enough.

Max is still dead asleep when I carry him into the restaurant, but he rouses a little when I get into the booth with him.

He pouts out his little lip and looks up at me with those big blue eyes.

"Want Mommy to sit with us," he pleads, and what can I do? Tell him no? Tell him that his mother's thigh next to mine might drive me crazy?

I nod to Lillian and she comes around the table to slide into the seat next to me. Max climbs over me to sit in her lap and sure enough, her thigh is socked up right against mine in the small booth.

I take in a deep breath and look at the menu like it holds the secrets of the universe, telling myself that everything's fine, it's just a dress. She's just a woman. The mother of my child, no less. I shouldn't be thinking of her this way for so many reasons.

Lillian, to her credit, doesn't make things worse, just pointing at the menu to show Max the kid's section—chicken fingers, burgers, et cetera.

He picks out a burger and fries and Lillian orders a half rack of ribs, which doesn't surprise me at all. She's always been a bit of a carnivore. The morning after we first hooked up she had eaten two plates of bacon and sausage at a breakfast bar we visited.

The server asks me three times what I want before I'm able to answer and I don't even remember what I order. I have to get my shit together.

Max chatters about the trampoline park and a little girl he met there that he declares is his "very best friend," and I'm struck by how sweet and loving he is. Lillian has done a good job raising him, and I can't deny that.

"I don't know how we'll get ahold of her parents for a playdate, Maxie, but if you ask Daddy really nice, he might take us back to the trampoline park."

Max looks at me with his bottom lip poked out and I chuckle.

"Of course we can go back. This weekend, after the wedding, if you like."

Max frowns and I curse myself inwardly. We haven't talked to Max about being married, exactly. He only knows that I'm his father and we're living together, and so far, he's just accepted it. He's adapted so well already that I haven't even thought about how it will look in his eyes.

"A wedding?"

Lillian nudges Max. "Remember, you helped me pick out a cake?"

Max's eyes widen. "*Oh*, does that mean you're marrying Daddy?"

Technically, she already has, but I don't want to confuse the little guy any more than he already is.

"Can I be the guy who brings the rings?" Max asks, munching on his fries, and Lillian looks at me, smiling softly.

"Of course you can be the ring bearer, buddy," I tell him, reaching across the table to thumb ketchup off his chin.

Max grins. "I'll be really careful with them, Daddy, I promise."

The last part comes out like "pwomise," and it's so cute I can barely stand it. Looking at him makes everything I've been going through with Lillian worth it, and this stupid wedding, too. I'm doing it for my parents, but now I realize that I'm also doing it for Max. He wants to see his parents together, wants to see us married, and of course, he does. He's grown up without me and it must seem like he's getting the family he should have had all this time.

The family he *would* have had, if Lillian had just told me.

My skin feels hot, and I wonder if the tips of my ears are red with anger as I glare at Lillian. She looks away, as if she knows what I'm thinking, and maybe she does. I'm not exactly quiet about the fact that I'm angry she took my son's first years away from me.

"I know you will, pal," I say softly, and Lillian hitches Max up on her lap. He wiggles around until he's wedged between us, and I'm grateful that she's not pressed up against me anymore. It makes me think things I shouldn't be thinking.

Whatever I feel for Lillian doesn't matter right now. All that matters is Max and getting this wedding over with.

12

LILLIAN

Saturday approaches much quicker than I thought it would, and at seven in the morning, I'm dressing a half-asleep four-year-old in a suit and vest.

Poor Max is so tired he keeps leaning on my shoulder, and I can't, for the life of me, get him buttoned up.

"Grayson!" I call, and he pops his head into the room, raising an eyebrow.

I laugh. "He's so sleepy, Will you hold him while I finish dressing him?"

"I don't know why we're dressing him now, the wedding isn't until two," Grayson complains, and I sigh.

"He insisted on it. He says if he's going to be the ring guy he has to look nice all day."

Grayson cracks a smile and it lights up his usually dark and stoic face. God, he's so handsome when he smiles. I swallow hard and look away.

He's all but avoided me like the plague in the last week, after the night he crawled into my bed, and it's been lonely. It's not like it's that different, because back at home I only had Max, but I also had Maria and my coworkers at the diner and the office. I've lost touch with everyone except for Maria, and it's been hard, especially since I'm about to go through an elaborate fake wedding.

The damage is done. We're already married and living together but apart, so I don't see why we have to put on this charade. He's told his parents that we're together, and they begrudgingly seem to accept it, so I don't know why they've insisted on this. I guess it must be some rich person thing —keeping up appearances and so forth. Grayson has warned me that the media will be there, and I don't know how I feel about being plastered all over local newspapers, but I guess I don't have a choice. I haven't really had a choice in any of this, and Grayson hasn't made it any easier.

Part of me had hoped that after the night he came into my room he'd realize that maybe we could talk things out, figure out how to co-parent without actually being married, but it seems like he's determined to keep things the way they are.

He's putting Max in the car before I can shock myself out of my thoughts, and I grab my purse and follow, just wearing a pair of sweats and a sports bra since I'll be getting dressed at the venue.

Max falls asleep in the car, and I sigh heavily, looking over at Grayson, who as usual, won't make any kind of eye contact with me.

"Why are we doing this?" I ask softly, not wanting to wake Max up.

"What do you mean?" he asks, as if it's a normal Saturday. He pulls out of the garage with one hand, hitting the button with the other to close it. "Would you have rather we got a sitter for Max today?"

I shake my head. "The sitter deserves today off since

she'll be keeping him overnight. I mean, why are we doing this wedding, Grayson? Why are we doing any of this?"

Grayson's shoulders stiffen and his full mouth thins as he grits his teeth.

"We've been over this, Lillian."

I hate the way he says my name now. It's so different than the way he used to. The syllables used to roll of his tongue, sweet and soft, the way he always acted with me. Now it's harsher, each syllable stilted as if I'm in some type of trouble.

"Have we? Because all I know is that you threatened to take Max and I said I'd marry you. We're married. I'm not going anywhere. Why do we have to stay married? And why in God's name do we have to have this big wedding?"

"Because it's what people want," he says quietly. "Because it's what *Max* wants. Don't you want him to grow up thinking that his parents care about each other?"

"Not if it's a lie," I say softly, and Grayson scoffs.

"Parents tell children white lies all the time. Santa Claus, the Easter Bunny... "

I don't say that this isn't a white lie. I don't say that I'm terrified that as Max ages, he'll realize that we're not in love, and that, in fact, Grayson can't stand the sight of me. What will that do to him? To know that his parents lied to him, that they were only together because of him?

"You've got it all figured out," I mutter, and Grayson looks at me from the corner of his eye for a moment before turning back to the road.

"I'm *trying,* Lillian."

I sigh. I suppose that's all I can ask of him, especially since I know how he feels about me and what I did. It's not that I expect to be forgiven, but I wish that we could at least come together as parents and figure things out for Max.

Surely, if I give it some time, Grayson will come to his senses and realize that we need to get an annulment. This can't be healthy for Max long term, but I understand why Grayson wants to be close to him. Grayson and Max deserve some time to get to know each other and bond, so for now, I just have to deal with what is coming.

Grayson's parents.

I shudder, and Grayson turns off the air conditioning. I don't tell him that I'm not cold, just terrified.

He pulls up to the venue, which is a large Catholic church at the center of town. The Saints of Something-or-other, I can't remember. This has all been a whirlwind. Just a couple of weeks of planning, and I only picked out a dress and the cake. It's been made very clear to me that this is Grayson's wedding, not mine.

An absolutely gorgeous brunette is standing near the front pew, putting a champagne-colored bow on the end, and she turns to look toward me. I feel a little intimidated. She's the kind of beautiful you only see in magazines, but as she gets closer, I realize that she looks like the female version of Grayson.

"Lillian!" she cries. "Finally, I get to meet you. And on my brother's wedding day, of all things."

She throws her arms around me, and I'm not much of a hugger but I hug her back, smiling nervously.

"Are you Grayson's sister?" I ask. I know that he has one, of course, he told me about her when we were younger, but he hadn't said much, just that she was the baby of the family and spoiled rotten. Grayson always had to work for his parents' approval, but he said that his sister seemed to have their affection and approval no matter what she chose to do.

"Meredith," she responds. "I'm sure he's said nothing but awful things."

I can't help but laugh, thinking that's mostly true.

"Siblings," I say, even though I don't have any of my own to commiserate.

Meredith smiles, taking a step back and looking me up and down. My cheeks heat up and I feel a little strange, being regarded by a woman who looks so much like Grayson. Those blue eyes of his must be strong in his genes, since Meredith and Max both have identical ones.

"You sure are pretty. Not his usual type," Meredith says mysteriously, and I have no idea what to say to that, so I just smile nervously.

"Thank you."

"Thank you for allowing me to be your maid of honor!" she chirps, and that's something I hadn't known at all. "When do I get to meet my nephew?"

Meredith speaks quickly and is a little demanding, intimidating just like her older brother, but she doesn't have the same bite that he or his mother do. She seems warm and she keeps her hand on my shoulder as she speaks. I guess she's not the worst maid of honor I could think of, and since none of my friends live in this state, it's fair enough that Grayson's sister would be part of the wedding party.

"He's going to be the ring bearer," I say proudly, and Meredith puts a hand to her heart.

"That's so sweet, oh my God. Mom has shown me pictures, he's the spitting image of Gray. I can't believe he's managed to hide you two from us for so long."

I blink. Had Grayson told them that we had been together all this time?

"Y-yes, he's very private," I manage.

I sure wish that Grayson had given me some kind of rundown to what he told everyone, because I'm flying blind here. I'm not surprised, he barely speaks to me, but I would think that he would want me to know what he'd said so that we could "keep up appearances," which he's so fond of.

"I'm just so glad that he found someone," Meredith gushes. "He's always been such a grump, especially in the last few years. The fact that he's been hiding how happy he is drives me crazy!"

I nod, having no idea how to continue this conversation. Meredith looks at her watch (a Rolex, from the look of it), and gasps.

"Shit." She does the sign of the cross quickly across her body as if to absolve her from having just cursed. "We've got to get you into hair and makeup."

She puts her hand on my lower back and ushers me into the back room, a small dressing room made just for weddings, it seems. I had expected a person to do my makeup, maybe another to do my hair, but there's a whole *team* of people in the cramped room, and they advance on me as Meredith pushes me inside.

She goes back out into the church, to presumably continue decorating, and someone starts buffing my nails while another woman tsks at the state of my hair.

"Don't worry," she says. "We'll take care of this."

I'm not sure what she's going to take care of and I have to admit I'm a little afraid I'll come out of this room looking like an entirely different person. It goes by in a blur as they chat amongst themselves and finish primping me.

When I look in the mirror, I blink rapidly, not believing what I see. My hair is perfectly coiffed, braided on both sides and hanging loose with big curls in the back. The light catches it just right so that the auburn color pops. I never even knew that makeup could look like this. They've given me false lashes over my already long ones, and it makes my brown eyes look larger, along with the natural eyeliner that matches my eye color and some reddish-brown eyeshadow.

As I'm staring at myself in the mirror, the woman who did my hair (no one introduced themselves, so I don't know how to address them) comes up behind me with the dress—a champagne-colored gown with a sequined top. I had picked it out but it had been from a selection of other dresses and they'd been swept away before I could get to look at it much. I'd done measurements but not actually tried on the dress.

Looking at it, sadness washes over me. This isn't how I imagined my wedding as a little girl, no matter how extravagant it is. I imagined that I'd get to pick out everything, make it my own, but this isn't *my* wedding, and that's clearer than ever.

"Don't you start crying on me yet, I haven't put on your fixer," the makeup woman warns sharply.

I laugh a little and it sounds fake to my own ears.

"No crying," I insist, and I won't. I won't shed another tear over Grayson Whitlock because he certainly hasn't shed any over me.

I undress, holding my hands over my breasts and standing there in just a pair of panties, and the hairdresser huffs and points at them.

"Take those off, too. No panty lines," she orders, and I gulp and do as I'm told, my cheeks hot with embarrassment at standing there naked.

As they all but manhandle me into the dress, I huff and suck my stomach in. I just *know* it won't fit, and I wonder if I've been eating too much between measurements. Eventually, though, something gives and the hairdresser begins to button the back as the makeup artist fluffs out the train of the dress.

I gasp when I see myself in the mirror. If I'd thought the makeup and hair was extravagant, it had nothing on the dress. Only the bodice is champagne-colored, with cream colored tufts of some silky fabric trail out from my belly-button to drag along the floor. It's beautiful, and it fits me like a glove, so well in fact that I wonder if I can even sit down in it.

I mention this to the hairdresser and she snorts.

"Wedding dresses aren't supposed to be comfortable, darling."

I tilt my head, looking at myself in the mirror. They'd done a good job, because I still look like me, just some princess version of myself. It should all be perfect, and tears shouldn't be stinging at the backs of my eyes.

I blink them back, the eyelashes feeling heavy on my lids.

"No crying!" the hairdresser says again, and I nod, running my hand down the bodice and liking how the acrylic nails they've put on (a simple French tip) tap along the sequins.

I'll look perfect in the pictures, and I know that's what Grayson wants.

That's all that matters.

13

GRAYSON

I dislike tailored clothes, no matter how often I'm required to wear them, and the black suit feels too tight across my thighs, the shirt too small across my chest. I prefer to be in casual dress or a simple suit, not something this expensive and fitted to my body. It feels like I'm in a cage of fabric and I keep tugging at my collar.

"Stop it," Lox says, smacking my hand. "You'll stretch out the collar."

"What are you, my mother?" I mumble, glaring at him. I cannot *believe* he isn't hungover, after he threw a bachelor party in my honor last night... one that I wasn't even invited to. There are pictures of him and a half dozen girls all over the local news.

"You should be so lucky," Lox snorts, peeking his head out of the door.

"Who are you *looking* for?" I ask grumpily, unbuttoning a couple of buttons on the silk shirt I'm wearing.

Locke gives me a wolfish grin. "No one in particular. Just checking out the attendance."

I scoff. "You're a dog."

"Listen, don't harsh my buzz." Lox pulls a flask from his jacket pocket and tips it at me before taking a sip. He offers it to me. I shrug and take a swig and start coughing immediately.

"God, what *is* that? It tastes like gasoline."

Lox shrugs. "I dunno. Something this girl from last night poured in there. It's getting the job done. What, I'm supposed to be *sober* at your fake wedding?"

He has a point there. Since I'd gotten so drunk with him last week, I told myself I wouldn't drink today, but it's becoming tempting. I've never been one to solve my problems with alcohol, but being numb seems preferable to the way I feel right now, all wide open and raw. I don't know what it is about this wedding that's making me feel so vulnerable, but I think it has something to do with my parents meeting Lillian and my whole family being here. The only time I thought I would get married was with Lillian. Then, of course, reality hit me in the face and I never thought I'd end up here again, have it happen like this.

When I thought once that I'd marry Lillian, I thought we'd elope, get married on a beach somewhere with our toes in the sand. I hadn't wanted to subject her to all this, and I guess I still don't, despite everything that's happened. Pulling someone into my dysfunctional family and my crazy life doesn't seem appealing, even if I can't stand her.

Unlike Lox, I hope my sister doesn't come around. She'll poke at me and poke at me, try to get something out of me about Lillian. Meredith has always been too nosy for her own good, but now I know she's just dying to get all the information.

My mother knows the truth, but I'd left it up to her to tell the rest of the family, and apparently, she had told them that I had been seeing Lillian for years and kept it under wraps. My mother kindly told me all of this in a text message a few days before the wedding, and I'm still reeling and trying to adapt.

I take one more swig of Lox's disgusting brew and hand it back to him. It's softened the edges somewhat, but it would take me a lot more than that to feel better, and I don't want to run the risk of the media knowing I'm drunk during my wedding.

Of course, my father had invited *everyone*: friends, family, clients, even the media. Especially the media. He's probably thrilled that I'm settling down. He's always hated my friendship with Lox and the fact that I'm unmarried after thirty.

"Family men land more clients," he'd told me, several times, until I was sick of it.

I sigh heavily and put on my suit jacket as I hear the music start. I haven't seen Lillian since this morning, when she was wearing that little sports bra like a shirt, and I'm hoping that the wedding dress leaves more to the imagination. It had been a struggle to keep my eyes off her trim waist and the swell of her breasts.

I push Lox out of the room. "Now, go find Meredith. You're walking her down the aisle."

Lox gasps. "What? I'll be walking down the aisle too? I thought I just had to stand there and pretend to not be drunk. If you'd told me that, I would have stopped drinking this an hour ago." He breathes out into my face and I wince. "Shit. Can you smell it?"

I shove a box of mints at him and he throws a handful into his mouth gratefully.

This is going to be a shitshow. I have no idea what the wedding party will look like or where I'm supposed to go because we didn't have a rehearsal of any kind. This was put together quickly for the sake of the media. My mother sure is good at covering things up.

I walk out, and the usher pushes me toward the door of the church proper. I stand in the doorway, uncaring about all the decorations and flowers. Meredith comes out of nowhere and pushes at my lower back.

"I'm getting real tired of people pushing me around," I growl, and Meredith rolls her eyes.

"God, if you're this much of a jerk on your wedding day I feel sorry for Lillian," she mutters, and points toward the altar. "You're supposed to walk down the aisle and stand over there."

I begrudgingly do as I'm told, nodding to the priest in greeting who just stares at me. Did someone tell him I'm a lapsed Catholic? I turn to stare down the aisle and see Lox grin as he offers his arm to Meredith. She takes it begrudgingly, and I can't help but notice how she turns her face to the opposite side. Looks like she doesn't want to get intoxicated by breathing the same air as Lox, which could happen just by walking next to him down the aisle. Finally, they split and Lox comes to stand next to me. Meredith takes her place on the other side of the altar.

It's not common to only have a maid of honor and best man, but it's not ridiculous for a smaller wedding. I don't exactly consider this wedding small, but at least the wedding party is. There are too many people sitting in the pews, and I don't recognize half of them. There's plenty of people on Lillian's side, although I know for a fact she hadn't invited anyone, so my mother must have been behind that, too. It doesn't escape me that her ability to put this together on short notice is nothing short of cunning. My mother is sitting in the front row, of course, watching me with judgmental eyes. I ignore her. I love my mother, but she's not the warmest person and she knows what this wedding really is.

I look down at my shoes, which feel too tight on my feet. I'm sure it's just the fact that I'm nervous and annoyed. The official wedding march starts, and I look up to see Max dressed in his little black suit and vest, identical to mine, walking down the aisle with a big grin.

Several of the guests ooh and ahh over him, and my chest swells with pride. He's holding the ring box tight in his small hand and he comes to stand next to me, smiling up at me.

"Best ring guy I've ever seen," I whisper to him and ruffle his hair.

Max nods, as if he knows and he's proud, and he hands the rings to Lox, who chuckles and fist bumps him. I look at Max while he looks down the aisle.

"Wow, wow," he says in an awed voice, and I follow his gaze.

My father, of all people, has his arm entwined with Lillian's and a hard look on his face, as usual. It takes me a moment to take her in, the way her hair is braided in front and falls loose down her back, the veil over her face, the dress which hugs every curve, cleavage spilling out from the top of the fitted bodice.

I lose my breath and have to hitch in the next one to continue to stand. Suddenly, it's like all the guests are gone and the only people in this church are me and Lillian. Something inside me seems to snap, my heart racing, and I break out in a sweat.

This isn't a real wedding, I remind myself. *She isn't really yours.*

My heart doesn't seem to be listening to my brain, though, and as she gets closer, I can smell her clean scent, that unique smell that's hers and hers alone. The veil covers her eyes and I can't make out her expression. She turns at the end of the walk and my father lifts her veil, kissing her cheek dryly. She smiles at him, and wonder of wonders, he gives her a small half-smile back, patting her hand before he detaches his arm from hers and walks over to sit next to my mother.

I close my mouth, realizing that it's open, and when Lillian stands in front of me, turns to me, the beauty of her face is almost too much to bear. She's beautiful without makeup, I can admit that, no matter how I feel about her, but seeing her like this, dolled up, my *wife*, it's overwhelming.

She licks her lips and I want to taste her mouth so badly I nearly lean down and do it right in front of the priest, but there's cameras flashing and I can't imagine what my mother would say.

She looks up at me under impossibly long eyelashes and I barely hear the priest when he starts to sing the opening hymn. I'd forgotten how long and involved Catholic weddings are, and I have no idea how I'm supposed to stand here looking down at this gorgeous woman who isn't mine for this long.

Lillian and I both mumble along to the words and it makes me laugh softly. She laughs too, too loud, and she covers her mouth with her hand. She looks so much like the Lillian I'd met when she laughs that it makes my heart ache.

I suffer through Meredith stumbling her way through the bible readings that precede the ceremony and finally, the priest begins to recite the vows.

"I do," I say when he finishes, and it comes out low and hoarse, too quiet almost.

Lillian's tongue comes out to wet her lips again, and I want to groan.

"I do," she responds, looking into my eyes the whole time, and something flashes across her face, something like longing.

Am I imagining this? Am I crazy?

Lox has to clear his throat to get my attention to hand me the ring box, and inside, my mother has snuck in my grandmother's engagement ring, an ornate and gaudy thing, but it'll do.

I manage to slide both the engagement ring and the band onto Lillian's finger without trouble, and she does the same, her small fingers trailing across mine while she does it. I can barely breathe, and I hate the way this feels.

I want her. Or maybe it isn't her that I want, but the woman I thought she was, years ago. I've never let go of that Lillian, and having this piece of her might kill me in the end. Suddenly, I want to run. I want to run straight to the court-house and get an annulment, figure out custody for Max, just get away from her in any way that I can. Panic is rising in my stomach, spreading across my chest.

You cannot do this again, I tell myself.

Then, it's over and the priest is wrapping things up and I'm not listening, turned toward the pews with a plastered on smile so that I don't have to look at Lillian anymore.

14

LILLIAN

I'm trying my best to listen to the priest but I'm shaken by what's just happened. It isn't the wedding, not really, but Grayson. His facial expressions have been so different than usual since he first saw me coming down the aisle, and I don't know how to feel about it. He'd looked right into my eyes during the ceremony, something he rarely does. I feel my cheeks heating up as the priest begins to speak and Grayson takes my hand. I glance up at him and he's looking down at me and I look away again quickly.

Don't read too much into this, Lillian, I warn myself.

"I've known Grayson since he was a boy, but I've only just met the recent Mrs. Whitlock," the priest begins, and I wince a little, wondering how the crowd will take it. They're silent, just watching, some people smiling from the pews. Grayson's parents aren't smiling, but it's not like I expected them to.

I don't want to think about that right now, so I try to focus on the priest even though all I can feel is Grayson's big hand wrapping around mine. How long has it been since a man held my hand? Years, probably. I went on a few dates in the past five years who might have led me to the car or something like that, but it was nothing like this. Grayson shifts and twines his fingers between mine and I know that I'm blushing visibly.

"The thing is, I was skeptical when Mallory asked me to officiate," the priest continues, looking over at Grayson's mother, who smiles politely at him. "I don't normally officiate without meeting both parties, but the Whitlocks are old friends and supportive members of the church."

I wonder if supportive is code for "donates a lot of money," and I assume it is, but of course, I keep my mouth shut. I've never been to a Catholic wedding, and I'm surprised that it's so involved, already. Grayson, for his part, doesn't seem bored, smiling and looking out at the crowd. He seems almost proud, but that has to be for the crowd and the cameras.

"I think God led me to accept the invitation, because as soon as I saw the way that Grayson looked at Lillian, I knew they were meant to be joined together in holy matrimony."

I glance over at the priest, surprised, but Grayson doesn't react, nodding as if he agrees. It's almost scary how he can flip his personality like this, on a dime. He'd been brash and rude to me just this morning, after all, and in front of all these people he's acting like we're really together. It stings just a little that he can be so cold in private and so warm in public. He's even fooled the priest.

"I've officiated for over seventy weddings in my long years, and I haven't seen a man so obviously in love in a long time." The priest's elderly face breaks out in a big smile, and I almost feel bad. He seems to truly believe that we're a real couple who is going to make it. "I wish you both the happiest years ahead."

A smattering of applause spreads through the church,

and a hymn begins to play, and I wonder if I'm supposed to sing again. Luckily, Grayson steps forward, tugging me along behind him, and I follow to the lobby of the church and outside, where we get pelted with birdseed. I can't help but laugh at how Max tries to catch the seeds as they fly at us, and then the au pair that Grayson has hired sweeps him up in her arms.

He pouts a little, watching us get into the limousine where we'll be taken to our reception, which will be held at a venue downtown—a historic building, from what the wedding pamphlet I'd pilfered earlier in the day said. It's a shame I have to read about my own wedding in a pamphlet instead of being involved with it, but it is what it is. I'm sure Grayson will want the marriage annulled soon enough, and this will all be no more than a memory.

I expect Grayson to break away from me the second the windows go up, but he stays next to me, keeps holding my hand, his thigh pressing up against mine. The train of my dress is bunched up in the floorboard.

Grayson looks straight ahead and I look over at him.

"That went well," I say, and he nods, his face blank and expressionless. I have no idea what he's thinking.

"The reception won't start for an hour," he states, and I clear my throat, not sure how to respond.

Then Grayson does something I would have never expected. He raps on the window three times and the driver rolls down the partition.

"Park up here," he orders, and the driver nods, rolling the partition back up.

The driver pulls into a parking garage, and I glace up at Grayson. To my shock, he puts his hand on the back of my head and leans down to kiss me, not hard and hungry like before but deeply, sticking his tongue into my mouth.

I gasp out a breath into his mouth, and Grayson groans against my lips, moving his hands to my waist where the fitted bodice is.

"Grayson," I manage as he begins to kiss down my neck. "What's happening?"

"You're my wife," he murmurs against my skin. "And you want me, right?"

My breathing becomes faster and harder. "Yes, but—"

"Then that's all that matters," he says, picking me up and depositing me in his lap. I straddle his hips, still confused, and he looks me right in the eyes.

"You want *me*?" I ask. "I thought that was just something you said when you were drunk."

"Drunk words, sober thoughts," he replies, leaning down to kiss the base of my throat, biting gently there. I tilt my head back for access.

"I thought you couldn't stand me," I breathe out, and then he rolls his hips up under me and I can feel he's hard through his slacks. I moan softly, trying to be quiet. I guess the driver probably has an idea what we're doing back here, but I don't want to make it too obvious.

"I can't," Grayson agrees. "You wrecked me," he says harshly, and his eyes are hard but hungry when he lifts his head from my neck. "But I still want you."

He lets out a grunt of frustration as he fidgets with the train of my wedding dress, ripping it in a few places as he bunches it up around my hips and when he sees that I'm bare beneath, he groans loudly enough for the driver to hear. Apparently, Grayson doesn't care if the driver knows what we're doing in the backseat.

"You can always tell me to stop," he murmurs right up against my ear, nibbling on my earlobe. He spreads his hands up my thighs, kneading the flesh there.

"I don't want you to stop," I whimper, and Grayson makes a noise in the back of his throat like a growl, sliding his fingers to my core, pressing his thumb against my clit so that I clench my thighs together with need.

"Thank God," he moans, shifting in the backseat to release himself from his slacks. "Fucking tailored suits," he mutters, and I can't help but giggle.

He stares at me for a long moment, his hands on his belt buckle. "Fuck, you're so beautiful when you laugh," he says, and I'm so shocked I don't know how to respond. Luckily, I don't have to, because he kisses me again, taking my breath. He's always been a good kisser but this is different somehow, hungrier than he's ever kissed me, urgent.

I slide back on his thighs to help him with his pants, and finally, fill my hands with his cock. When I wrap my fingers around him, he thrusts into my hand. Impatient, he slides my hips forward and when I move my hands, he slides his member along my lower lips, dragging it through my wetness.

"Fuck," he curses.

"Fuck," I agree, unable to say anything more. I know that I shouldn't be doing this, that it's a bad idea. I know that it'll be harder than ever not to fall for him again, but it's been so long since I've been touched. It's been so long since somebody wanted me like this.

Grayson doesn't waste time, taking hold of my hips and picking me up slightly so that he can slide inside of me, and I clamp my hand over my mouth to muffle my moans.

He moves one of his hands to my wrist, roughly moving my hand away.

"Want to hear you," he grunts.

"The driver—" I start.

"Fuck the driver," Grayson growls, and something about

the way he says it sends a shock of pleasure up my spine. "Want to hear you when you come for me."

He's deep inside me at this angle and I start to roll my hips. Grayson cries out and clamps both hands down on my hips.

"Wait," he gasps, and I smirk, liking how desperate he looks.

"What's wrong?"

"This won't last if you do that," he says, looking up at me with hooded blue eyes. "I want this to last."

I can't help the way my walls flutter around him, and Grayson moans loudly.

"Naughty girl," he says, and it reminds me of the day in the bathroom and my skin heats up, something building in my lower abdomen.

He begins to move inside me, thrusting up from beneath me, and I dig my nails into his shoulders.

"Grayson," I gasp, and he stops moving his hips while I whine.

"Say it again," he orders.

"Grayson," I repeat. "Grayson, please."

"Please what?" he asks.

"Please fuck me." I look right at him as I say it.

"Are you begging me, naughty girl?" Grayson murmurs, and I nod. He shakes his head. "Need you to say it."

"I'm begging you, Gray, *please*," I whine, at the verge of tears because I just need *more, more, more*.

I need him so badly I'm not sure I'll recover after we're done, honestly, but I don't care. I just need him to move right now, or I'm going to explode.

Grayson grins at me and starts to roll his hips, dragging against a sweet spot inside me that makes me see stars. He groans and buries his face in my neck, kissing me open-mouthed there, dragging his teeth along my skin.

"Lillian," he murmurs, and the sound of my name on his lips catapults me toward orgasm and I begin to rock my hips in time with his thrusts. It's almost embarrassing how quickly I'm reaching my peak, but I haven't been made love to in so long. Not that I would exactly call this making love. It's hungrier than that, more urgent.

"I'm coming," I warn, gasping, and Grayson just fucks me harder and faster, kissing down my neck.

"Thank God," he groans. "I'm so close. You're so tight and wet."

I start to moan loudly, and to muffle the sound, I kiss him, sticking my tongue into his mouth. Grayson kisses me back, hard and eager, not deep and exploring like before. I can feel his thrusts getting sloppy, feel him pulse inside me, and I know he's close.

"Want you to come inside me," I whisper, knowing that will help him along. "Make me yours."

Grayson has always been possessive, and he used to love it when I said things like that in bed. Evidently, he still does, because he clamps down on my hips, thrusting up as deep as he can go, and releases inside me just as I'm orgasming. I open my mouth in a silent scream and Grayson loops his hand around my throat, squeezing slightly. It only makes the orgasm stronger, last longer, and I'm all but whimpering when he moves his hand and kisses along my neck.

I feel dazed, out of it, and I blink slowly at him.

Grayson smirks. "You good?"

"Better than good," I slur, and then clear my throat, my cheeks flushed. "But.."

Before I can tell Grayson what I'm thinking, before I can

tell him that we shouldn't do this again, Grayson's phone begins to vibrate in his pocket and he curses.

"It's Mom," he explains. "We're late for our reception."

He barks out a laugh and picks me up with his hands on my hips, hissing as he slowly pulls out of me. I adjust my dress the best I can and push back the tendrils of hair that have escaped from my braid in the front.

"How do I look?" I ask, and Grayson's smile turns wicked.

"Like you've been fucked, and fucked well."

I put the back of my hand to my hot cheek, looking away from him.

"Shut up," I mutter. "Let's get to the reception."

Grayson doesn't hold my hand on the way back, but he doesn't move to his side of the backseat, either, resting comfortably next to me, his shoulder brushing mine.

I have no idea what the hell is going on with him, but I'm not complaining.

15

GRAYSON

Something about taking Lillian in the limo has made me feel instantly better, and it's improved my mood so much that I can't seem to stop smiling at the reception. I can blame it on the champagne glass that keeps getting refilled all I want, but I know it isn't that. It's the fact that I've figured things out with Lillian. I don't have to like her, but since I want her so badly, the sex will help matters. It can make me feel close to her without me actually having to be with her.

I've been missing Lillian Brooks for going on five years, and now, I don't have to, anymore. It doesn't mean that I'm falling back in love with her, not at all. It just means I have needs, and it happens that I'm not attracted to any other women as much as I am to Lillian. This marriage is the perfect situation, honestly. I get to be with my son and I get to have regular sex with my wife and the mother of my child without risking heartbreak again.

This isn't a good idea, something in the back of my head warns, but I don't heed its advice, just sipping my champagne. The thing is, I feel better than I have in years, and I'm not going to let my head take that away from me.

Meredith comes up to the table that Lillian and I are sitting at and grabs Lillian's hand.

I look over at her but Lillian's been quiet ever since the limo and I figure she's a little overwhelmed. I know that she wants the same things that I do, though, so I'm sure she'll come around.

"Your dress," Meredith exclaims. "It's ripped."

My sister glares at me and Lillian giggles softly. She's been partaking in the champagne too, maybe heavier than I have, and I frown, not wanting her to get too drunk. We still have our wedding night ahead of us, after all.

"Maybe you should switch to water," I suggest, and Lillian's brown eyes flash when she looks up at me.

"Maybe I'll get another glass of champagne," she shoots back, and I sigh, wanting to roll my eyes. Lillian has a penchant to be a brat when she feels like she hasn't got control of things, and I suppose that this wedding had been totally out of her control.

"Yeah," Meredith agrees. "You ripped her dress; let her have all the champagne she wants."

My baby sister drives me crazy, but I have to admit I'm glad that she seems to get along with Lillian. I know that my wife doesn't have any friends in this area, and I've taken her and Max away from everything they know. I want her to make connections here, because after all, we're going to be married forever.

Catholics don't divorce, and I can't very well get an annulment with a clear conscience after what just happened in the backseat of the limo, so this is it. I'm a married man, and things are going well despite our past. I'll have to talk to Lillian more about it, but being husband and wife with benefits definitely works for me.

I find Lox at the appetizer table, shoveling down lobster puffs, and I tilt my head toward Lillian.

"I think this is going to work out fine after all," I say.

Lox raises a thick eyebrow. "Yeah? Did you consummate the marriage already?"

I don't answer, just grin and finish my champagne, and Lox whoops.

"Finally! It's about damn time you got laid, Gray. Maybe now you'll stop being such an *asshole*."

I frown at him. "I'm not an asshole."

Lox shrugs. "Not to me, but I've heard things."

I roll my eyes and look around for Lillian, but I don't see her and Meredith anywhere.

There's a hand on my arm and when I turn, smiling, I see a woman I recognize: Elizabeth Banks.

My mother tried to set me up with her a couple of years ago, and we'd went out two or three times. I'd even kissed her, but in the end, I couldn't bring myself to go any further. I can admit that I wasn't over Lillian at the time (and maybe I'm still not over her), but Elizabeth is a good girl, and I had liked her. I just hadn't been in love with her.

Elizabeth's smile looks pasted on. "I thought the wedding was lovely," she says. "And your bride, too."

I keep smiling at her. "Thank you, Elizabeth. It's good to see you."

"I was surprised when your mother invited me—I thought that you were still a bachelor, and I had no idea about your son."

Elizabeth pauses, fiddling with her designer purse, as if she isn't sure what to say next.

"I kept it pretty under wraps," I admit softly, not wanting to cause her any pain. I know that she had stronger feelings for me than I ever had for her because she'd told me so when I broke things off. "Lillian and I broke up for a while, so I promise I wasn't cheating on her when you and I... ."

I trail off because it seems like her smile is fading.

"You don't have to lie to me, Grayson," she says, something harsh in her tone. "I know that you must have been seeing her then, too."

I frowned. "I wasn't, Elizabeth. I promise you."

"So you just didn't like me?" she asks, her voice breaking, and I reach out to put a hand on her arm. She pulls away.

"That's not what I meant," I say gently, and I'm grateful when Lox clears his throat.

"I think you should go find your wife," he says. "She's talking to your mother."

Shit. I know that my mother and Lillian won't get along, so I need to defuse that situation.

"I'm sorry, Elizabeth. I have to—"

She nods. "I know. You have to go. Marital duties and all that."

I give her a wry smile and take off in the direction that Lox is pointing. My mother and Lillian are standing in the hallway of the venue and their conversation seems heated.

They both sound loud and like they're arguing, although my mother's voice is usually pretty calm, even when she's upset.

"What's going on?" I ask, and Lillian's brown eyes shoot to mine. They're flashing with anger, just like earlier, and then she looks away.

"I'm talking to your new wife. Getting to know her," my mother says easily, and at the same time, Lillian speaks.

"Nothing," she says in a mutter, and I frown.

Something's definitely going on here, but neither of them seems to want to admit it, so what can I do?

My mother trails into the venue to sit down and eat, and Lillian won't look at me, even when I take her hand.

I lean down so that I can whisper in her ear.

"What's going on with you?"

Lillian shrugs. "I'm just tired," she mumbles, but I don't know if I believe that.

"It's time to cut the cake," I say, and I lead her over to the cake table where everyone is taking pictures and watching. Lillian shrinks away from the attention but I pull her forward, in front of me, and we feed each other cake.

I smash it into her face and she finally cracks a smile and does the same to me, smearing it all over my chin. Instead of giving her a napkin I pull her toward me and kiss her in front of everyone. There's a raucous of applause as the guests watch, and I hope it'll be plastered all over the front page of a newspaper.

It'll stop the rumors about Max in their tracks and deter any guy who might want to go after Lillian, and that's killing two birds with one stone.

When I pull away from Lillian, something spreads across her face before her expression shutters again, and I wonder if I might have my work cut out for me.

16

LILLIAN

Mallory Whitlock is a stern, unfeeling woman, or at least that was my first impression of her back when I was dating Grayson.

I'm surprised that she doesn't approach me at the wedding, honestly. She's just been giving me death glares the whole time I've been at the reception, and between that and what just happened with Grayson, I feel grumpy and exhausted. I'm physically exhausted from the wedding and emotionally exhausted from the stress of it all. I've had no idea what's going on all day, and I'm so confused about what Grayson wants from me now that I can't even start to think about it.

"You wrecked me," he said. What does that even mean? Does he mean because I took Max away from him? He has to. He didn't care about me, not really, back then. He never indicated that we were anything other than a casual fling, and so when I left, I didn't know that he'd care.

I'd just found out that he was only playing with me while my heart was totally his. He was supposed to be married to someone who had class, someone who was rich, someone in his class. In other words, anyone but me. I had to save myself the humiliation, even if there was nothing I could do about my broken heart. So, I'd left. A clean break. But a break nonetheless. And it had wrecked me.

Now, everything's changed, and Mallory Whitlock is walking toward me with that same stoic, cold look that Grayson gets.

"Lillian," she greets, something icy in her tone, and I force a wan smile.

"Mrs. Whitlock," I respond, and she shakes her head.

"*Mallory*," she insists. "I'm your mother-in-law now, aren't I?"

I grit my teeth. "I suppose so."

Mallory looks around as if checking to see if anyone is watching us, and when she sees that they aren't, she leans forward, close to my ear.

"I thought you left town," she hisses in a low tone.

"I came back," I snap back.

"I didn't know you were pregnant," she accuses, and I scoff. *Neither did I at the ticm, but whatever.*

"Would it have changed anything?"

"It would have changed everything," she says fiercely, and I know that she's good with Max, that she seems to care about him, but the way she'd acted toward me back then... I can't forgive her.

"You don't have to worry, *Mallory*." I make sure that my tone has the same ice in it that hers does. "Despite what happened between us back then, Max and I aren't going anywhere." I wonder if she'll see that as a threat, but she doesn't seem to, offering me a stiff smile with too many teeth.

"What's going on?" Grayson's voice breaks through my anger and I look up at him.

"Nothing," I mumble, just as Mallory gives some excuse. We part ways and the cutting of the cake all goes by in a blur. I don't know how to feel about him being so close, about him being so... different. He had said that he couldn't stand me, but he's acting like we're actually married, and it's confusing to me.

What does he want from me? Just someone to warm his bed? I don't know if I can do that more than once without falling even more in love with him. I'm afraid to do that, afraid to offer him my heart again, especially because I know how he feels about me. I don't even think he hates me at this point, more that he's indifferent to me and my feelings, but for some reason, he still wants me.

Meredith comes to sweep me away into the bathroom, handing me a bag with a pair of high-waisted shorts, a T-shirt, makeup wipes, and a truly insane amount of condoms and lubrication. I blush when I look through it.

"Didn't think you wanted another baby just yet," she says happily. "And I hope the shorts are okay. I got your size from Mom and I thought you'd want something a little more casual to leave for your honeymoon."

Honeymoon? Grayson has mentioned his parents wanted us to have a long weekend away, but surely he knows nothing about it will be remotely close to a honeymoon, and I don't want to leave Max with the sitter for too long. Surely, it's just for show.

"Y-yes," I stutter. "Thank you so much, Meredith."

She hums, waving her hand dismissively.

I take her hand and look into her face. "No, really, Meredith. You've been so kind to me and... everyone else hasn't been."

Meredith frowns. "Who hasn't been nice to you? I'll set them straight."

I laugh, shaking my head. "Never mind. I just wanted you to know that I appreciate your kindness and I hope that we can be friends."

"Not friends," Meredith says, and my face falls. She takes my other hand and squeezes them both. "We're sisters now."

Tears spring to the backs of my eyes at her kind words and I blink them away.

"Sisters," I agree.

I've always wanted a sister, so her words sting a little given that this isn't a real marriage. I'm sure that Grayson will figure out that we need to divorce sooner rather than later, and then I won't be able to see Meredith anymore. I shouldn't get too attached, but she's one of the only one in this town that's been kind to me.

Meredith turns me around and begins to unbutton my dress, and when it falls free, I sigh in relief. It's so fitted that it's constricting my chest, and I finally feel like I can breathe again. I normally would be a little embarrassed to be naked in front of a woman I barely know, but Meredith seems so sweet that it doesn't bother me too much to get dressed outside of the stall. My dress won't fit in the small stalls, anyway.

"God, that's so much better," I groan, and Meredith laughs.

"Wedding dresses aren't made for comfort," she agrees.

I cock my head, curious. "Are you married?"

Meredith blanches. "God, no, bite your tongue!"

I laugh. "Not in the cards for you?"

Meredith shrugs. "Just haven't met the right guy, I guess."

I nod solemnly. "I know how that is." She looks at me with a raised eyebrow, and I clear my throat. "Before I met Grayson, of course."

She seems to relax, and I figure I've convinced her. Why am I speaking so openly with her, anyway? She's Grayson's little sister, and she's likely to tell him anything I say. Or maybe not. He hasn't indicated that they're particularly close or anything.

When Meredith and I come out of the bathroom, we run into her father, who hugs her tightly before turning to me.

"Welcome to the family, Lillian," he says, and although he's got the same blank expression that Grayson gets sometimes, his smile is bright and warm. He seems like the polar opposite of Mallory, at least when it comes to me.

Grayson had often complained about his father's coldness and lack of emotional availability, but in my opinion, Mallory is much worse.

Meredith trails off with her father after I thank him and shake his hand, and I walk back over to the cake table, where Grayson's drinking yet another glass of champagne. He has a lot of nerve telling me how much I can drink when he's all but chugging from the bottle.

I grab myself another glass out of spite, even though my head is spinning slightly already. I'm not much of a drinker. In fact, this is the first time in years I've drank this much.

"I think it's time we get out of here," Grayson says, and his best friend, Lox, gives me a wolfish grin. Grayson frowns at him when he winks at me, but Loxton doesn't seem to care. I giggle. Loxton's funny, and I like him.

Grayson's face goes all shuttered and he takes my hand a bit roughly. He's changed into a pair of board shorts and designer slides with a button up short-sleeved shirt.

Everyone comes out of the venue and watches us as we get into the limo again, and to the driver's credit, he just smiles at us instead of accusing us of fucking in the backseat of his car.

"Where are we even going?" I say tiredly when the limo pulls off.

"The beach," Grayson says easily. "My parents booked us the honeymoon suite."

I look at him. "Did you always plan on us sleeping in the same hotel room?"

Grayson shrugged. "It's just a bed. I figured I'd sleep on the pull-out couch."

"And now?" I ask, leaning a little closer to him. Maybe it's a bad idea, but I can't help myself from preening under the new way he's treating me.

"Now what?" he asks, looking out the window.

I frown. "Now you're not going to sleep on the pull-out couch, right?"

Grayson looks at me. "Just because we're sleeping together doesn't mean we're going to actually *sleep* together."

What the hell is that supposed to mean? Is he trying to say that he'll fuck me but he won't fall asleep in the same bed with me? I huff out a breath, offended, and look down at my hands. Grayson doesn't offer an apology, and I'm not surprised. I'd be shocked if the man has ever apologized for anything in his life.

We don't arrive at the hotel for half an hour or so, and I'm silent the entire way. Grayson is too, leaning against me as if he's tired, and I suppose he must be. I'm certainly exhausted and all I want to do is lie down in the big bed at the hotel. Sex is the last thing on my mind.

Apparently, it isn't the last thing on Grayson's, though, because after we check into a truly extravagant hotel and walk into the suite, he puts his hand on my waist.

"Not now, Grayson," I say irritably, and he grunts something unintelligible.

"Don't flatter yourself, sweetheart," he drawls. "I just

wanted to ask if you're hungry. I could barely eat at the reception with everyone talking to me."

I haven't eaten at all, my belly full of nothing but champagne, and my stomach growls when he asks the question.

"I guess I'll take that as a yes," he says, and pulls out his phone to order. I have no idea what he's getting but I don't care, my belly feels like a bottomless pit right now.

I walk out onto the balcony, looking out across the beach, and the breeze sweeps my hair back from my face. I close my eyes, enjoying it, and Grayson comes up behind me.

Once upon a time, he would have slid his arms around my waist, kissed my neck, but now he just stands stiffly beside me.

I've been thinking how differently he acted at the wedding and reception, but now he isn't acting differently at all. He's acting like the same Grayson who's been ignoring me even though we live in the same house.

"Why are we here, Grayson?" I ask, feeling exhausted.

"What do you mean? It's our wedding night," he says, as if it's a stupid question.

"Keeping up appearances," I say, and Grayson nods.

"Keeping up appearances," he repeats, and then slides his gaze to mine. "That doesn't mean we can't enjoy ourselves."

"What about Max?" I ask. "He shouldn't be without us very long."

"It's just another day. He's got his au pair and my mother."

It's a struggle to keep my face from wrinkling at the mention of his mother. His sister had been lovely, and his father hadn't been bad, either, but his mother? No, thanks.

I guess it makes sense, we need to have some kind of

honeymoon to appear like we're in love and actually want to spend time together, instead of just being stuck together the way that we actually are.

"And you want a repeat of the limo?" I ask, looking down over the balcony at the pool below.

"Don't you?" Grayson asks, and nudges my shoulder with his, almost playfully. "It was fun, wasn't it?"

It *had* been fun; he was right about that. It had been fun, but it had also been confusing. I don't know if I can continue having sex with Grayson and keep things the way they are. I don't know how I'll handle it. As much as I want him, I can't separate my heart from my body. I guess that he can, but I can't. Men are better at that kind of thing, I've heard.

I don't say anything, looking out over the pool.

"Lillian?" Grayson calls, and I finally turn to look at him.

"One more time," I say firmly. "And then we focus on Max, on being parents."

Grayson looks down at me with those sharp blue eyes of his. "One more time," he agrees, and leans down to sweep me off my feet, carrying me bridal style into the bedroom.

I gasp and giggle, and the smile he gives me lights up his whole face.

17

GRAYSON

As much as I want it to be just sex with Lillian, as much as I don't want to get my heart involved, I have to admit that the second time in the hotel is a lot different than the rushed way we'd had sex in the limousine.

This time, it's less rushed, sweeter. I take my time with her, touch her the way I'd wanted to before she left. Her skin is soft beneath my hands and I kiss the reddish marks the fitted wedding dress left on her.

"You looked beautiful today," I tell her, and Lillian's eyes widen in surprise. "I did?" Her voice is low and soft, as if she doesn't believe me.

I hum against her inner thigh where I'd been kissing her and her legs open up beautifully for me.

Before I can answer her, the aroma of her sex takes me over and I bury my face in it, finding her clit and bumping my nose against it before sliding my tongue into her entrance. Lillian cries out, clamping a hand over her mouth. I reach up, tsking in the back of my throat, to grab her forearm and pull it away from her face.

I lift my head. "Wanna hear you," I mumble before latching on to her clit, sucking until I have to take a deep breath through my nostrils, until her thighs are trembling around me. When I slide two fingers inside her, she's hot and slick, and it isn't long before she comes, clenching around my fingers as I moan against her.

I want to line up between her trembling thighs, slide inside of her, but I'm still wearing jeans and someone's rapping on the door—room service.

Lillian squeaks and burrows under the covers and I can't help but smile, heading to the door to tip the room service attendant and wheel in the food.

She peeks her head out of the covers when the smell of breakfast fills the room.

"Bacon and sausage," I tell her, pulling off the dome covering the food.

She opens her mouth and I feed her a link sausage. She moans, almost louder than when I had my face buried in her.

"Would you and the breakfast like to be alone?" I ask dryly, and Lillian laughs. It's loud and open, like I've rarely seen it, and it makes her look even more beautiful. My heart stutters in my chest, and I push all the emotion back down, let my face shutter my expression.

Lillian digs into the meat heavy breakfast while I eat the hashbrowns and pancakes. Breakfast had kind of been our thing, back when we were dating. We'd spend the night together and then the next morning I'd order breakfast in. Sometimes we'd go out, but I liked it best when we could eat together in bed, with the long line of her thigh pressed against mine.

She eats now and I watch her, watch her mouth chewing

and the graceful line of her throat, and it makes my chest ache. This is too much. I shouldn't have given in to what my body wanted, shouldn't have fucked her in that limo and I certainly shouldn't fuck her again the way I want to—slow and easy, taking my time, breathing her in.

All of that is a bad idea, but it's all I can think about. I grab her ankle, wrapping my fingers around the delicate bones of her foot, spreading my fingers up her calf.

Lillian draws in a sharp breath. "Grayson," she breathes, and I feel light-headed hearing my name on her lips.

"Lillian," I respond, and she bites her lip, looking at me with those wide, doe eyes of hers.

"Do you think we could ever be friends?" she asks, and that's about the last thing I expected to come out of her mouth.

I look at her for a long moment, my eyes searching her face. "No," I say honestly, and I don't think it's because I hate her but because it would kill me to be just friends with her and not be able to touch her. It would be some exquisite kind of torture.

Lillian's face falls and even I can't ignore that. I hate it when she's hurt, it hurts me too, somewhere deep down in my bones, a pain I can't get to in order to heal.

"I don't think we should do this anymore," Lillian says, and I swallow hard.

"Do what anymore?" I ask, even though I know what she means. I'm being deliberately obtuse because I don't want her to tell me that I can't touch her again.

"The sex, Grayson. It's confusing."

"Confusing for whom?" I ask her, tracing my hand up her thigh but she stops me, putting a hand over mine.

"Grayson," she says, in a low, almost scolding tone, and

anger boils up in me again. It's not anger at her for saying no, but anger at the way I feel rejected by her. The way it makes my stomach turn.

"So, you'll just be celibate?" I ask. "Because I said no men."

Lillian shrugs. "I guess I have no choice."

I let out a long breath. "I don't want to control you, Lillian, but this has to look real."

She looks up at me from under long eyelashes. "I know that."

"This has to *be* real, for all intents and purposes."

"It can be real without the sex. We've consummated it. It's done," she says firmly.

I want to curse. I want to tell her that it's not just consummation I want, that I want *her*, body and soul, but that doesn't matter anymore. I can't forgive her, anyway, and getting back together for real would just be bad for Max when it inevitably ends.

Everything ends, I remind myself. *Nothing lasts forever.*

I nod slowly and throw her one of my T-shirts from the nearby luggage. "You should put something on, then," I tell her, and my words sound harsher than I mean them to.

Lillian clutches my T-shirt over her breasts, and I turn my back, heading into the bathroom for a *very* cold shower.

When I exit the shower, I don't bother putting on my clothes, lying on the pull-out sofa in the other room in just a towel. I can feel Lillian's eyes on me.

"You should probably put something on, too," she says dryly, and I smirk, turning to look at her.

I shrug. "I wear what I want. You'll just have to get used to it."

Lillian heaves out a sigh and I rub a hand across my face

to hide a smile. Just because she says no sex doesn't mean that I can't tease her, right?

⁓

THE TRIP back to the airport is long and quiet, with Lillian pressing her head against the window, looking out at the beach that we never visited. We stayed in the hotel the whole time, and we didn't even have sex, not really. I'd tasted her, though, and that's enough to keep me wanting her, glancing at her legs in the high-waisted shorts she's wearing.

They aren't inappropriate in the slightest, but it seems like anything she wears is inappropriate on her frame. I'm just attracted to her, and nothing seems to stop that, even the fact that she ruined my life, broke my heart, took my child. I still want her no matter what, and that's going to drive me crazy the more I'm around her.

My plan is to bury myself in Max and in work, to not think about her or how she felt wrapped around me in the limo, how she tasted with my tongue on her.

Max is ecstatic to see both of us, and when he asks for a group hug with big blue eyes, neither of us can say no. Lillian's breasts push up against my upper arm and I squeeze my eyes shut, focusing on Max.

He chatters about his time away from us, telling us about all the board games he and Grandma played, and I'm shocked to hear that my mother sat down and played with him. She'd certainly never done that with me.

My mother had been standoffish at best and cruel at worst in my childhood, depending on if I met her nearly impossible standards or not. I'm glad that she's acting differently with Max, but I can't deny that it makes me feel a little rejected.

I'm feeling rejected all over the place, lately, and I can't stand it. At least I have Max, who loves me despite only knowing me for such a short time.

I'll focus on being a father to Max and my work, and I'll forget about Lillian.

18

LILLIAN

Grayson Whitlock is driving me crazy. I don't know if he means to be so attractive when we arrive back home from our faux honeymoon, but it's definitely affecting me. He comes through the hallway with just a towel slung around his hips, goes for early morning runs shirtless in just a pair of basketball shorts. He returns sweaty and smirking at me as I stare at him, and I blush and look away.

I cook breakfast for us every morning, even though it's bittersweet because that's the meal that Grayson and I had shared together more than any other when we were together. Grayson begins leaving earlier and earlier for work and missing breakfast, so it ends up just being Max and me.

Max frowns the fourth morning that Grayson leaves early. "Why does Daddy have to work? Isn't he rich?"

I laugh. "He is, but he got that way by working very hard," I tell our son.

I don't know how true that is. I'm sure that nepotism played a role in why Grayson moved up the ranks in his family's company, but he was a brilliant marketing executive all on his own.

"You won't ever have to go to work, right, Mommy?" Max asks, and I sigh.

"I don't know, buddy."

I miss marketing myself, having gotten a degree before working at a low-level company for years, just as the receptionist. I'd never had the time as a single mother to find a good job. I wonder if I can do that now, look around for something that I could do at least part-time. I'm going a little stir-crazy being stuck in the house all the time, as extravagant of a house as it is.

"I guess one day I'll have to go to school," Max muses, and I smile, ruffling his hair.

"Not for a few more months. Don't grow up too quickly on me."

After breakfast, Max gets distracted playing Uno with the au pair, Holly, who's a sweet older woman. I wish she was Max's grandmother instead of the one he has. Mallory Whitlock is a force to be reckoned with, and I don't want to have to deal with her any more than I already have.

I clean up a bit in the kitchen, although we have a housekeeper named Esther who comes once a week. I can't help myself; I'm used to cleaning up after myself and also, it gives me something to do.

Grayson comes back in from work earlier than usual, picking up Max at the door and swinging him around.

"What do you say we go and play outside for a bit, bud? I got that new swing set all set up yesterday."

"You did?" Max cries, running out the back door to get to the yard.

Grayson chuckles, looking after him, and then he looks over at me.

"How was your day?"

"Boring," I respond, cranky.

"You're in a mood today," Grayson mutters.

"I'm stuck around the house all day doing nothing, Grayson. There's only so much mommy stuff I can do without wanting to do something else. I'm used to working two jobs and now—"

"Now, everything is being taken care of. Just relax," Grayson says idly, removing his suit jacket, and I huff out a frustrated breath.

"I don't want to relax, Grayson. I want to get a job," I say firmly, and he glares at me.

"We made ground rules when we started this, Lillian—"

"And there shouldn't be rules like that in a *real* marriage, Grayson. You said you wanted this to be real in every way that counted, and you know that I've never wanted to be a housewife."

"So, you want to get a job?" he asks with a sigh, seeming tired.

I cross my arms over my chest. "Yes, I want to get a job."

"You'll work at Goliath Marketing," he says, as if the matter is settled and I just stare at him.

"You want me to work for your father's company?"

"For *my* company," he corrects. "I want you to work with me, so that I can... keep an eye on things."

So that he can keep an eye on *me*, he means. What does he think, the second I get out of the house and am around males, I'll become a slut?

"I don't need you to keep an eye on me," I say stubbornly. "I'll get a job somewhere else."

Grayson throws his suit jacket on the couch with a groan. "Fine, Lillian, I'll put you in lower level marketing and you'll barely even see me. Okay?"

"I don't want you to hire me. I want to get in on my own."

He rolls his eyes. "God, you're stubborn. Fine. Apply

online. You've got the credentials if not the experience. I'll tell my assistant, Sheila, to pull your application." When my mouth opens he holds a hand up to stop me. "Just so that you can get an interview. No more than that."

I finally nod slowly, and we walk outside to watch Max playing on the swings, sweeping down the slide with a whooping noise. I laugh and film some of it, even when Grayson goes to push him on the swings and tries to get down the slide, getting stuck halfway down. Max laughs so hard he nearly wets himself, so we go in to give him a bath as it's nearing dusk.

Grayson strips off his shirt as we enter the house, throwing it on the floor. I hate how the throws his things everywhere, just assuming that someone else will clean it up, so I pick it up.

"Doesn't this have to be dry-cleaned?" I ask, and Grayson smirks at me.

"Yes, wife," he drawls, and it's playful rather than cruel and makes my heart race.

Later, I disappear into my room, changing into one of the nighties that I bought with Grayson's credit cards after he had that weird breakdown about my old, ratty T-shirts. The nightie is a little too short and barely covers the tops of my thighs, but Max is in bed and I'll just be lounging around the living room, anyway.

I'm tired of being in that bedroom by myself, and since this is my house too, I plan to actually utilize the space. Grayson's fresh out of the shower and wearing just a pair of gray sweats when he comes into the room.

I've got my legs up under me on the couch, watching some vapid reality show and putting in my application on my laptop, one of the few possessions I'd brought with me.

"That thing looks like a relic. Buy a new one with that

card I gave you," Grayson says flippantly, as if it didn't cost me a week's paycheck to buy this a few years ago.

"I don't need a new laptop," I say, and Grayson snorts.

"You will if you're going to start work."

I worry my bottom lip between my teeth. He's right, unfortunately, and there are programs for photo and video editing I'll need to upgrade.

"Are you sure you don't mind?"

He waves a hand dismissively. "That card is one I designated for anything involving you and Max. If he needs new clothes? Use it. If you need something for work? It's yours. It doesn't have a limit, so don't worry."

I gape at him. I'd never thought about using it up to the limit, and knowing that it's an unlimited credit card is a little insane. I didn't even know those existed!

"Th-thank you," I stutter, surprised, and Grayson shrugs.

"It's my job to take care of my family," he says simply, without looking at me, and walks toward the bedroom, leaving me just as confused as ever.

I don't know what he wants from me, but I'm determined to start a career so that when this inevitably falls apart, I have a backup. I need to start saving some money, and I refuse to take anything out of Grayson's account to do so.

I diligently answer all the questions on the application, being honest about how I hadn't worked in the industry except for a receptionist, and I'm surprised to see I get an email back within a couple of hours.

Goliath Marketing is pleased to interview Lillian Whitlock for the position of marketing executive. Please arrive fifteen to twenty minutes before your scheduled interview time.

The address is listed to the office, and I wonder if Grayson works there or in a different building. I'm sure the human resources building isn't where he spends most of his time. I send a text to Holly to ask her to watch Max the next morning for the interview, my heart racing with excitement. It's been a long time since I'd interviewed for a job, and even longer since I'd interviewed for one that I'd actually enjoy.

When I head back into the bedroom, I notice that the door to Grayson's bedroom is open, and I peek in to see him lying on the bed, shirtless, one hand sprawled across his waist. The moonlight is streaming right on him, so I can see the trail of hair below his navel, disappearing into his waistband. I swallow hard and shut the door, hurrying back to my room.

I have my work cut out for me, living with a man this attractive and not being able to be with him.

19

GRAYSON

I throw myself into work after we return from our sad excuse of a honeymoon, and spend all of my free time with Max. Lillian is still traipsing around the house in those little nighties, and I almost regret telling her to buy them.

I manage by taking *very* cold showers every night and trying not to look at her, no matter what she's wearing. I've realized by this point that it isn't what she's wearing, or what makeup she has on, it's just that she's gorgeous, and particularly gorgeous to me. It's like no matter what she's done, I still want her, so I have to keep my mind off it.

Luckily for me, we've just landed a huge deal with a law firm and we're doing all their marketing. I've been paired up with a bright young marketing executive by the name of Charlotte Richards, and she's brilliant. I have to admit that I wouldn't be able to do my job as well if it weren't for her, and we're working together quite closely. She's a few years older than me, and she's been in the business just as long, so I feel comfortable with her.

We go to dinner after a long night at work on Thursday, and when I get home, Lillian's pouty, clearly in a mood. She and Max are sitting at the dinner table, and I realize that she's made pot roast, a meal that I've repeatedly told her is my favorite.

It's congealing on the table, and I swallow hard, wondering if she's angry with me. I shouldn't care, given what she's done to me, but I don't like the look of disappointment on her face.

"Mommy got a job!" Max crows the instant that I walk into the kitchen, and I look over at Lillian. She blushes slightly, looking away.

"Just wanted us to have a nice family dinner," she says quietly, her voice sounding hurt.

"You should have told me," I start, coming closer to her, and she takes in a deep breath and then gives me a shrewd look.

"I wanted it to be a surprise." She narrows her eyes. "You already had dinner, I assume?"

I nod and ruffle Max's hair. "Time to get a bath, kiddo. Go pick out your pajamas."

Max obediently heads off to his room, and I look at Lillian but she's still looking at the floor.

"I'm sorry I missed dinner," I say earnestly. "I really didn't know you were planning it. If you had texted me—"

"Weren't you busy?" Lillian accuses, shooting her gaze to mine.

I stared at her. "I was at dinner with a colleague, it was business related."

"Hmm, was it? You sure smell a lot like perfume for it to have been a business dinner," she snaps, and it slowly dawns on me.

"You're jealous," I accuse, a smile spreading across my face. Lillian had never really been the possessive type, even when we were together, and she'd never shown a sign of it after we'd been married. I can't deny that it makes me happy, especially since the thought of her with someone else drives me nuts.

"I'm not jealous," she hisses, throwing the congealed pot roast in the trash and beginning the dishes, even though Esther will be coming in the morning.

"You're *very* jealous," I say with a chuckle, coming up behind her and she groans, throwing plates into the dishwasher. I grab her wrist. "Take it easy on my plates, would you?"

Lillian finally looks up at me, her bottom lip poking out slightly.

"It was really just a business dinner?"

"It was really just a business dinner," I promise, and god, I want to kiss her. I want to kiss her so badly I almost lean down and do it right there.

"I found my jammies!" Max announces, and I slowly drop Lillian's hand.

I lean down, close to her ear. "Come to my room after Max is in bed. We can celebrate," I whisper.

Lillian shivers but doesn't respond, and I can't stop smiling when I go to Max to put him in the bath.

He splashes water all over me, so I remove my shirt and toss it in the laundry basket in his room before reading him a story, getting into bed with him because of his pleas for cuddles. I could never deny him anything.

Max is fast asleep within half of a Dr. Suess book, and I disentangle my limbs from his and head toward my room. I'm surprised to see that Lillian is standing in the doorway, dressed in one of those nighties.

"You said we were going to celebrate," she says, and holds up a bottle of champagne that I'd had chilling in the fridge ever since I started this new account. She holds two glasses in her other hand.

"I was saving that for a special occasion," I tell her, and Lillian raises an eyebrow.

"Isn't this a special occasion?"

I swallow hard. I'd asked her to come here but I guess I hadn't exactly thought it through. I walk past her into the room, and when I turn around, she's discarded the nightie and stands there bare-breasted in only a pair of panties, just as lacy as the nightwear.

All the breath goes out of my body in one breath as I stare at her.

"Help me celebrate, Grayson," she says in a low voice, popping the champagne, and some of it dribbles between her breasts. I want to lick it off but I restrain myself, watching as she pours two glasses.

She sips hers and I chug mine before leaning down to kiss her, eager.

She pulls away from me and I groan. "I thought you wanted to celebrate."

"I do. That means champagne," she says, taking a couple of steps back from me.

I frown and pour myself another glass. "Drink up," I tell her, and she finally finishes her first glass. "That's enough celebrating," I announce and pick her up, dropping her on the bed as she giggles.

When I cover her body with my own, kissing her deeply, she makes a noise into my mouth.

"Grayson," she says against my lips, and I hum out a response. "We need to talk about this."

I grunt, pulling her panties down and off. "Do we?"

"We do," she insists, keeping her legs closed even as I put one hand on each of her thighs to spread them.

I lick my lips, having to force myself to look up at her eyes instead of down at her body.

"It doesn't have to mean anything, Lillian. I'm attractive. You're attractive. We want each other, right?"

Lillian frowns. "Right, but we have a child."

"I don't understand what this has to do with Max," I groan.

"The way we react to each other affects him, Grayson. We need to have some kind of truce."

"Isn't this enough of a truce?" I ask, raising my eyebrow.

She snorts out a laugh. "No. I need you to forgive me."

I shake my head instantly. "I can't," I say, and it isn't because I want to be cruel. It's because I honestly don't know if I can forgive her.

"Then you need to at least be civil," she says.

"I am civil," I argue, and Lillian sighs.

"I'm serious, Grayson. We need to have some kind of understanding if we're going to be sleeping together and be parents."

"Parents with benefits?" I ask with a laugh, and Lillian grins.

"I guess so. I don't see anyone else; you don't see anyone else."

"Naturally," I drawl. "And we keep the peace for Max's sake?"

Lillian nods. "Exactly."

I think about it for a moment, looking down at her pretty face. "I can do that," I assure her, and then, she lets me spread her thighs.

I moan, looking down at how slick she is when I spread her, and push down my gray sweatpants, freeing my cock. It bobs up against my stomach, hard and ready, and when I guide myself into her, Lillian cries out.

I put a hand over her mouth. "I usually love to hear you, sweetheart, but we don't want to wake up Max."

Lillian curses, rolling her hips up against me, and I grin, thrusting into her slowly. She likes it hard, fast, and rough, so when I fuck her deep and slow like this, I know it's torture.

Her nipples have pebbled in the cool air conditioning and I move my hands to grab her breasts as I continue to fuck her, working the peaks between my thumb and index fingers. She makes a mewling sound in the back of her throat, quieter.

She's so hot and slick around me, clenching her muscles as she gets close. I grit my teeth so that I don't burst inside her too quickly, slowing my thrusts just slightly. She whimpers.

"Please, Grayson, harder," she pleads, and who am I to deny her? I'm close to the edge anyway, after teasing her, so I snap my hips into hers, fucking her harder and riding her rougher while I pull at her nipples with my fingers.

"You feel so good," I groan, thrusting harder and deeper inside her, and just like always, it's like when I'm inside her nothing else matters, not the way she hurt me, not the years I spent trying to find her, not the fact that she took Max. All that matters is that she's here and she's mine, at least for this moment.

The second I spill inside her, I figure I'll regret it, but instead, I kiss along the side of her face, let my heart swell the way it wants to, don't push all my emotions down.

"When you're in my bed, you're mine," I murmur, and that's the way it feels, that's feels right, somehow.

"I've always been yours, Grayson," Lillian says, half-slurred with pleasure as she continues to pulse around me, and my heart feels like it might break all over again.

I clear my throat and pull out of her slowly, lying on my back and breathing hard.

"You should go," I say hoarsely, and Lillian doesn't look at me, just nods, and I don't like that her eyes are wet but I don't know what to do about it. If she stays, I might say something stupid. I might ask her to stay longer, to spend the night. I might tell her that I want more.

Even if that's true, I can't give her more than I'm giving right now. I'm still too hurt, my heart still too broken.

Lillian grabs her nightie off the floor and slides it on before exiting the room in her bare feet, taking the bottle of champagne with her and shutting the door.

I close my eyes against the sound of the door shutting.

Fuck.

20

LILLIAN

I don't know what I expected. Did I expect Grayson to tell me he still loves me, ask me to stay in his room with him all night? Did I expect him to tell me he wants to be my husband for real instead of just in name only?

I chugged the champagne, sitting in a half full tub of water in my bathroom. I'm already feeling tipsy but I don't want to be just tipsy. I want to be *drunk*, for the first time in years. I can't do this, sleeping with Grayson and still loving him but not getting a single crumb from him other than sex.

I know that he still hates me. He told me that he can't forgive me and I have to respect that, but it doesn't make wanting him any easier.

After about half the bottle is gone, I decide to call my best friend, reaching over to grab my phone from the floor and missing twice before I grab it.

"Lillian?" she answers. "It's after midnight, are you okay?"

"No," I sob. "I started sleeping with Grayson again."

"He's your husband," Maria says dryly.

"No, you don't understand," I say, wiping my face and sniffling. "We're only married in name."

"What are you talking about, Lil? I know you said it was temporary but—"

"We did it so that Max wouldn't be a scandal," I try to explain in my inebriated state. "We're supposed to just be doing it for show, but after the wedding, we slept together and... I still love him, Maria. I can't help it!"

"Look, I don't know what is going on but I know I need to come visit," Maria says firmly. "Put down the liquor—"

"Champagne," I correct her with a hiccup.

"Whatever, just put it down, and this weekend I'll come and take you out to dinner and for drinks. We can go dancing, like we used to when Max was little and you had that great babysitter. What was her name?"

"Erica," I say, taking in deep breaths through my nose to calm myself. "I miss her."

"Get some rest, babes. I'll text you tomorrow with plans."

My head spinning, I agree and hang up, getting out of the bath with some effort and drying off. I don't bother putting on clothes, just stumbling to the bed and burrowing under the covers.

I'm out like a light the second my head hits the pillow.

I WAKE up with cotton in my mouth and my head feeling like it's going to explode. I manage to wash my face and brush my teeth before Max comes bounding into the room, peeking his head into the bathroom.

"Dad just left for work, said that you might sleep in. Are you sleeping in, Mommy?'

"Not anymore," I say, groaning, and Max laughs and starts to jump on my bed.

Luckily, Holly the au pair comes to collect him, giving me and the discarded bottle of champagne a sympathetic look. Bless her.

I don't start work until Monday, so at least I have the weekend to get over this hangover. It's Friday and I vaguely remember talking to Maria and her saying that she's coming to visit. Sure enough, she's sent me a text asking for my address. I squeezed one eye shut against the headache and texted her the address with a sigh. I hadn't asked Grayson's permission, but he'd said over and over that I could use his credit card for whatever we needed, and I need this. I need time with my best friend and to celebrate my new job.

I spend my time napping and reading up on marketing since I've been out of the loop for a few years, and Holly handles Max for the most part. He asks her to help him make me some tea for my belly and she helps him make me some ginger tea to bring to me.

"You're so sweet," I tell him, kissing the top of his head as he cuddles with me in the bed. Holly leaves us be, and when Grayson returns home from work, that's where we are, Max asleep on my lap.

I hear him come in with the key in the lock and he pops his head in after just a few moments.

"There he is," he murmurs, loosening his tie. "How's your hangover?"

I'm embarrassed that he knows I was drinking after he'd all but kicked me out of his bedroom, but it hurt to be rejected that way.

I clear my throat. "Fine, Max made me some ginger tea and I feel a lot better."

"Good." He leans against the doorjamb. "I was thinking maybe we'd all go out to dinner tonight, as a family."

I shake my head. "I've got plans."

Grayson's shoulders stiffen. "What do you mean, plans?"

"My best friend is coming to visit. She wants to take me out," I tell him, and his eyes narrow.

"Just your best friend?" he asks.

"I don't think she's bringing her husband, so yes, just my best friend," I say dryly. "Why, did you think I was going to a strip club or something?"

Grayson sighs and his shoulders relax finally. "No. I won't stop you from going out, either."

I raise an eyebrow. "I didn't think you would. You said you didn't want to control me."

"I don't," he shoots back, and it almost feels like we're having an argument.

"So, you'll stay home with Max, then?"

Grayson shrugs. "Maybe I'll go out after he's in bed. Meet up with some friends."

"With Loxton?" I grin. "Tell him I said hello."

"I'll do no such thing," Grayson grumbles, and I laugh as he walks back toward his room.

Maria lands at six in the evening so I kiss Max's head and get dressed in a pair of jeans and a simple white blouse to go and pick her up from the airport. Grayson doesn't stop me, and when I see her at baggage claim, I give her a big hug.

"You look pretty good for someone who downed a bottle of champagne last night," she teases.

"It wasn't a whole bottle," I complain, and she laughs. I help her with her luggage and she widens her eyes at my car.

"Is this yours?"

I nod. "Grayson says he's going to get a minivan, one of those new BMWs, but this is plenty for me and Max. I keep trying to tell him."

"You married a billionaire, Lillian. You should try to enjoy it."

I bite my lip. "That's the thing, Maria. It's hard to do that when your husband hates you."

"We have so much to talk about," she announces as she slides into the passenger seat. "Do I get to see Maxie before we go out?"

"He'll be home with his father. We should get home before his bed time."

Sure enough, Max is wrestling Grayson on the floor of the living room when we get home, yelling and laughing as Grayson pins him and tickles him.

Grayson looks up at us and Maria widens her eyes again, giving me a look as if to say "this is your billionaire husband?"

I ignore her and pick up Max.

"Aunt Maria!" he says, and launches himself into Maria's arms.

Maria laughs and kisses his temple. "It's good to see you. Andy misses you."

Andy is Maria's elderly pug, who adores Max despite Max pulling his ears and tail all the time.

"I miss him, too," Max pouts, laying his head on Maria's shoulder.

"He's sleepy," Grayson mouths to me, knowing that if Max hears the word "sleepy," he'll freak out and start to yell that he's not at all tired.

I nod and take Maria to his room so that she can lay him down on his bed.

He asks her to tell him a story about Andy and she tells

him about the time Andy got his head stuck in the staircase. Max laughs himself into a fit before he falls asleep.

I smile at Maria and Max as Maria extracts herself from his bed. I've missed my best friend terribly, and seeing her with my son just makes me happier that she's here.

"Now," Maria whispers. "It's pre-gaming time. I bet your husband has an excellent bar."

I don't actually know what kind of bar Grayson has, but she's probably right.

I plan to sneak into the kitchen while Grayson is in the bedroom but I find him in the kitchen at the table, drinking a small glass of scotch.

Damnit. How am I supposed to have a girls' night out and gossip to my best friend when my husband is watching me like a hawk?

21

GRAYSON

aybe it's unhealthy to go out just because I want to keep an eye on what my wife is doing, but I can't help myself. After she and her friend get ready in her room, giggling like schoolgirls after a few shots of my most expensive tequila, she comes out in a white, skintight dress that shows ample cleavage and her long, shapely legs.

There will be plenty of guys out that hit on her, that want to take her home, and I'm certainly not letting that happen. I know that I shouldn't still feel so possessive over her, but after we started sleeping together again, it's only gotten worse. She's mine, whether either of us likes it or not, and I refuse to let anyone else take her.

If I'm going to hate her and love her at the same time and deal with that, I can't deal with other men on top of it.

Lillian hasn't indicated that she's even interested in seeing anyone else. In fact, she's said that she doesn't, but I don't trust other men. Especially when she looks like that.

I don't interfere with what they're doing, just watching and laughing at them occasionally.

Maria is wearing a red dress, contrasting with Lillian's

white one, and they're a good-looking pair of friends, I have to admit.

"What club are you going to?"

"Dinner first. Your treat," Maria says dryly, and I chuckle.

"Fair enough. Where next?"

"None of your business," Lillian snaps.

I raise an eyebrow in her direction. "Fair enough," I say again.

Maria looks over at Lillian but she doesn't say anything.

"I'll hire a car to take you so that you can both drink," I offer, and Lillian narrows her eyes.

"Is that so you can keep tabs on me?"

I raise my hands in defense. She seems angry, and I'm not sure why. I know that I had sort of kicked her out of my bedroom last night, but she's the one who had insisted we be "parents with benefits."

"Just trying to be nice," I say, and Lillian crosses her arms over her chest and doesn't respond.

"Thanks for the car," Maria says. "And dinner and drinks. You're footing the bill, of course."

"Of course," I drawl with a grin. I rather like Maria, even though Lillian's being difficult.

The car is driven by a good friend of mine named Alexander. He's worked with my family for nearly fifteen years, and he'll tell me where they go if not exactly what they do.

All I need to know is the club they're going to afterward, after all.

I stay at home until Alexander calls me around ten that evening, telling me that Maria and Lillian are at The Edge, a club nearby that a lot of younger people go to.

I call Loxton, of course, because he's the only one who would go with me on an errand like this.

"Gray!" he answers, too loud, his words a little slurred, and I curse under my breath.

"You already drunk, Lox?"

"Only a little," he complains. I hear a lot of background noise.

"Where are you?"

"That dive bar you took me to. Met a cute little bartender here, but she's not working tonight," he says glumly.

"Good. Need you to come out with me to The Edge tonight."

"The Edge? You looking for some college girls to pick up?" Lox asks with a laugh.

I snort. "Absolutely not. I'm looking for my wife. She went out with her friend and I just want to keep an eye on her."

"Of course you do," Lox says, but then he pauses. "I'm always down to go to The Edge. Meet you there in fifteen?"

Thank God for Loxton. He's always willing to indulge in my dumbest ideas. It's probably the reason we're still friends. I'm pretty strait-laced, but every once in a while, I make bad decisions, and it's always Loxton that helps me.

I call another driver, informing Holly that I'll be out late. I make it to The Edge in just about half an hour, and I can see Lillian and Maria waiting in line.

Before thinking about it, I grab Lox, dragging him by his arm, and slide the bouncer a few hundreds, pointing toward the girls in line.

"We would like to get in now, please," I say, and when the bouncer looks up at me and Lox, he seems to recognize us, his eyes widening.

"Ladies," he calls, and Maria and Lillian come to greet us, Maria nods her greeting to Loxton and he does the same to her.

"I'm not going to let you ruin my night, Grayson," Lilian hisses.

"Wouldn't dream of it, sweetheart," I say easily, smiling.

She's cute when she's pissed off. She's cute all the time, to be honest. It's one of the things I can't stand about her, at least now.

"You didn't tell me there'd be a blonde here," Loxton accuses.

"She's off-limits. Married. But I'm sure you can find a few replacements to entertain yourself with if our company bores you at any point in the night," I offer.

He blinks. "You're right."

I laugh and order a round of shots on my tab to keep Lillian from running up my black card. Not that it matters, there's no limit. I guess I just want to pay for a few of her drinks. I told the truth when I said that I didn't want to control her, but I do want to keep tabs on her. I can't help it. We're married, but we're not officially together, and I worry that she'll meet someone else. It's one of the reasons I hadn't wanted her to get a job. At least she'll be working at my company, where I can keep an eye on her.

I drink contentedly with Loxton as Maria and Lillian talk, but when they head off to the bathroom and I lose track of them, I frown, setting my jaw as I look around.

"Where did they go?" I ask Loxton, but he's flirting with the female bartender.

I curse and head toward the women's bathroom and that's when I see her–she's pinned up against the wall by some big guy, and her brown eyes wide and a little frightened.

"Lillian?" I call, and her eyes dart to mine and she tries to move from under the guy.

He protests. "Hey, where you going?"

"The lady is with me," I say in a low voice, and the guy frowns and steps back from her. He's bigger than me, wider, but that's okay. I've been taking karate since I was ten years old, and I've never been in a fight I didn't win, including bar fights.

It wouldn't look good on the news, but I'm ready to swing anyway. Luckily, another guy, less drunk, comes up behind him and grabs him by the arm to haul him off.

"Sorry, he gets like this when he's drunk," the friend says, and I don't respond, staring at the guy who had been pinning my wife against the wall.

I turn to Lillian when they walk away. "Did he touch you?" I ask her.

"N-no," she stutters, looking up at me. "He didn't hurt me. It's just like this sometimes, guys in clubs."

"Not when I'm around," I growl, and take her hand, dragging her into the alley outside.

"Look, Grayson, I don't want to do this with you," she groans. Her eyes are a little glassy and I wonder how much she's had to drink. At least as much as me, and my head is a little fuzzy.

"Do what with me?" I ask, and I'm angry. Furious, even, but not at her, at that guy who had thought he could touch her.

"I don't want to fight with you."

"Who's fighting?" I ask, reaching down to caress her cheek. "I just want to make sure you're okay."

"I'm okay," she says softly, searching my face, and I can't help myself. There's too much liquor in my system to refrain from leaning down to kiss her, soft and sweet.

She kisses me back, sliding her tongue between my lips. Her arms wrap around my neck, fingers playing in the hair at the nape of my neck, which I've let get way too long in the past few weeks.

"Lillian," I whisper against her mouth.

"Hmm?"

"Unless you want me to take you out by the dumpsters, you're going to have to stop kissing me."

"What if I do?" she moans into my mouth and I curse.

"Dirty girl," I tease, kissing her again and she melts against me. "Fuck, I wish I had my car."

"Take me here," she manages. "Up against the brick, I don't care."

"You're going to be the death of me, Mrs. Whitlock," I groan, and she giggles.

"Why don't I just meet you in your room later? After Maria falls asleep," I murmur. She bites her lip and I want to kiss her again, but instead, I put my hand on her lower back, leading her back into the bar.

22

LILLIAN

I have to admit that I'm drinking more than usual, but it's not until the world begins to spin on its axis that I realize I've drank *too* much. I brace my hands on the bar in order to keep myself upright and then Grayson takes me by the upper arm.

"You okay?" he asks and I don't miss the slur in his own voice, but he's a lot bigger than me and can presumably hold his liquor.

"I'm okay," I say, making an effort to make my words stay clear instead of slurred and blinking to keep my focus. My vision is close to doubling, so it's time to switch to water.

Maria has her head on the bar, nearly asleep, and Grayson looks over at her and laughs.

"I think it's time to go home, don't you?"

Grayson walks me to the car while Lox all but carries Maria to the car that Grayson ordered for us. Lox rides with us to his place, which is a mansion that rivals Grayson's.

"I'm never drinking this much ever in my life," Maria slurs as the car starts riding again, and I burst out laughing.

"I'll be sure to remind you of that."

Back at the house, Maria manages to stumble inside by herself while I need a little help, stumbling in my heels. I don't wear them that often, and particularly not when I've had too much tequila.

Grayson walks me to my room, smiling at me as I wrestle out of my dress and get into bed with Maria. He goes back to his bedroom, a complete gentleman, and I pout, looking up at the ceiling.

Maria snores, and not quietly and lady-like, loud, like a saw cutting through a log. After a few moments, when the world stops spinning, I get up and stumble toward Grayson's room, bracing myself on the doorjamb when I knock.

"Come in!" he calls.

I open the door too wide and it bumps the wall behind it.

"Oops," I giggle.

"What are you doing here, Lillian?" he sounds tired but not angry, maybe even a little amused.

"Maria snores," I pout. "Can I sleep here with you?"

I'm already crawling into the bed before he answers and he chuckles softly.

"All right, but no funny business," he warns.

"Why not?" I ask, snuggling up under the covers.

"Because I'm drunk," he teases. "Wouldn't want you to take advantage of me."

I snort out a laugh and get closer to him, wishing that he'd put an arm around my waist the way he used to. As if he read my mind, he does, slinging his heavy arm over my hip and waist.

I think about the way he kissed me in the alleyway, the way he'd had his hands on my hips, led me into the bar with his hand on my lower back. I want that. I want all of that, all of the husband stuff and all of the Grayson stuff. I just want *him,* so badly it makes my heart ache.

"Are you ever going to forgive me?" I ask, my face pressed into the pillow.

He's quiet for so long I think at first he's fallen asleep.

"I don't know," he says softly. "I want to."

"I want you to, too," I say, and I'm conscious enough to add, "for Max's sake."

Grayson stiffens but he doesn't respond, and I fall asleep before I know what hits me.

The next morning, I wake up to an empty bed. Grayson's already left for work and when I get up to go into the kitchen, I see that Holly has already fed Max breakfast.

Maria is in my bathroom, throwing up, and I pop my head in the doorway to check on her.

"You good?" I ask, and she retches.

"Absolutely not. Why in God's name would you let me take tequila shots?"

"You're the one that ordered them!" I say, laughing.

"Your rich husband paid for them," she mutters, lying down on the bathroom floor.

I sit down on the floor next to her. "I slept with him last night."

She lifts her head. "Again?"

"No," I shake my head. "Just slept, for the first time since we dated."

"Did he cuddle with you?" she asks.

I tilt my head, curious. "Does that matter?"

Maria huffs out a breath and sits up slowly, crossing her legs under her. "Of course it does."

"What does it mean if he did?"

"It means there's a chance that he's still interested," she says, and my throat tightens.

"God, I wish," I mutter.

"What happened between the two of you, anyway?"

I shrug. "What always happens. It was casual and I got a job somewhere else, so I left," I lie. "I didn't figured out I was pregnant until later. And by then I didn't know how to get ahold of him after."

I don't like lying to my best friend, but the truth is my secret to keep, and I plan to keep it that way. Besides, I really didn't know I was pregnant when I left Grayson.

"And he's mad about it?"

"I guess," I murmur. I honestly haven't talked to him about it much, just because he's been so standoffish and I've been worried about what might happen. I don't want him to snap and try to take Max from me because he's angry.

"Have you talked to him about it?" Maria asks, as if she's caught on to my train of thought.

"Absolutely not," I say, as if that's ridiculous.

Maria snorts. "Then no wonder you're freaking out about having sex with him again. You're in a marriage and you know nothing about how your husband is feeling. You should talk to him."

"Maybe," I sigh. "In the meantime, do you think you can eat some breakfast before your flight? Our au pair makes a mean sausage biscuit."

Maria mock gags and I laugh, but in the end, she manages to get down a biscuit and some orange juice and looks less green at the airport. She tells Max goodbye and he pouts a little, but doesn't cry, content to play with Holly while we're gone to the airport.

I hug her tightly at the gate. "I'm going to miss you," I tell her, tears welling in my eyes.

Maria sniffles. "Don't make me cry. I'll miss you too, but I'll come to visit soon."

"I could come to visit you," I suggest.

Maria wrinkles her nose. "Why would you do that, you live in the big city and have the rich husband. Let me live vicariously through you. I married for love like an *idiot.*"

I sniffle and laugh at the same time, waving at her as she goes through the gate to the plane.

I will miss her terribly, and maybe she has a point–maybe I should talk to Grayson.

23

GRAYSON

Lillian is acting different when I get home from work, and I'm not sure why. I suppose she might just be hungover, but it seems different. She's biting her cuticles and her bottom lip and pacing around the house, even after Max is in bed.

"You want to order in?" I ask her, and it feels strange to ask such a domestic question to this woman that I still have so much resentment and anger toward.

"Sure," she responds shortly. "How about Chinese?"

"This is an incredibly tense conversation about what to eat for dinner," I murmur, ordering our favorites on my phone and tossing it to the side. "What's up with you?"

"I guess I'm just homesick," she says.

"That wasn't your home," I comment, not angry, just telling the truth.

"I know," she responds, looking up at me with big brown eyes. "I guess I just miss the way that things used to be."

Me, too, I think but don't say. I miss the way that we used to be together, the way she looked at me then, the way I felt about her. I miss Lillian, the one I thought I knew, but this

Lillian who left me and took my child is a different woman altogether.

I hum in response since I'm not sure what to say.

"What are we doing, Grayson?" she asks.

I shrug. "We're doing what I said we would. We're married, keeping up—"

"Appearances," she finishes and there's an edge to her voice.

"Appearances," I agree, not sure what else she wants me to say.

"And the sex?"

"Casual," I respond, although it's been anything but casual. "We both have needs."

"We could get our needs fulfilled somewhere else," she suggests and I feel my shoulders stiffen.

"Is that what you want?"

Lillian looks at me for a long moment and my heart races.

"No, not really."

"Then why even bring it up?" I ask, exasperated.

She sighs. "I don't know. I guess I just feel like I'm missing out on something. Something that I could have if we weren't... doing this."

"You want to date? Is that what this is all about?" I accuse.

Lillian rolls her eyes. "You don't have the right to get jealous, Grayson."

"Damn right, I do. You're my wife, aren't you?"

"In appearance only, right?" she accuses, crossing her arms over her chest.

"In more than appearance," I say in a low voice. "I don't know what it is you want from me, but you know this is more than just appearances."

"Do I? Do I know that, Grayson? You don't talk to me. We're either fucking, arguing, or just being parents and there's no time to talk about me and you."

"You want to talk about me and you?" I ask, sitting up straighter, my teeth gritted. "You want to talk about how you left me with our baby in your belly? You want to talk about how devastated I was? How I looked for you for years?"

"You didn't," Lillian whispers.

"I did. I looked for you. I spent tens of thousands of dollars looking for you. It was like you disappeared off the face of the planet. And now you ask me if I can *forgive* you? If I can just be okay with you dating someone else?"

"What do you want me to do, Grayson? Do you want me to get down on my knees and beg for your forgiveness?" she asks, sliding off the couch and dropping to her knees.

I curse and look away from her as she crawls toward me, putting her hands on my thighs.

"Lillian," I start, but I don't know how to finish my sentence. Just the feeling of her hands on me is making my head feel light. I can't believe she still does this to me, after everything I did.

"Tell me what to do, and I'll do it, Grayson," she says softly. "I just want to go back to the way things were. I want us to be a real family."

I look down at her, my eyes searching her face. I've never felt so conflicted as I do right now.

"I don't know what you can do. I don't know how to fix it," I say honestly, my voice hoarse. "All I know is that I still want you, after everything."

"You do?" she asks, her eyes welling with tears.

I groan and sweep her up, pulling her into my lap, grinding against her. "Can't you feel how much I want you?" I murmur close to her ear. I want to turn things sexual again, turn things casual, because this is too much. This hurts too much.

"Grayson," she breathes, my name on her lips sounding almost religious, and I push her nightie up her hips, now grateful that I'd asked her to buy them.

I've changed into my sweats so it's easy to push them down, free myself and slide my erection against her sex, letting her slickness lubricate me.

Lillian gasps and digs her nails into my shoulders, but I don't mind. I like thinking about her in the shower later. I think about her all the time, anyway, so I might as well have a reason.

As I guide myself into her, Lillian's thighs tremble and she kisses me, hard, sliding her tongue into me the way I'm sliding into her.

"Fuck," I murmur against her mouth. "You're so wet."

"You make me this wet," she mumbles back. "I only want you, Grayson."

I surge up beneath her, unable to help myself, thrusting up into her while she lets out a series of little moans. She's already slowly clenching her muscles around me so I know that she's close, wish I had taken more time with her, wish this wouldn't be over as quickly as I know it will.

"Lillian," I moan, and I want to say, *"you're the only one I've ever wanted,"* but it doesn't matter because I can't be with her, not in the way that she wants. I haven't forgiven her and I don't know if I can. It helps to hear that she wants me, that she wants to do this for real, but it doesn't erase the years I spent heartbroken, the years I spent looking for her, the years I missed with Max.

She seems to know this, tears streaming down her face as she rides me, rocking her hips back and forth, bracing her hands on my chest. "Grayson," is all she says. "Grayson, Grayson," just repeated over and over.

It's enough and I cry out when I spill inside her after she comes, after I feel her nails dig into my chest and her thighs tremble around me.

She climbs off me almost immediately, even as I'm panting and trying to clutch on to her hips.

"I'm sorry," she says, something liquid in her voice, and she leaves the room on shaky legs.

I curse and lean forward, putting my elbows on my thighs. I don't know what to do now. I hate this. I hate that she wants me the same way that I want her. I hate that she's implying that she still loves me, that she ever did in the first place. I hate that she's here and I can't have her, not in the way I want. And it's not because of her. It's because of my own broken heart.

I've hated her for so many years but I've loved her just as much, and I'm realizing that now. Not that it matters. The part of me that hates her is still loud and angry, and there's no way that I can reconcile it.

I'm fucked.

24

LILLIAN

I know that sleeping with Grayson and then immediately apologizing and leaving isn't the best luck, but I didn't know how else to do it. I can't do this anymore. I can't be with him anymore without sacrificing everything that I am. I still love him, and I can't deny that anymore, not even to myself.

I still want him, body and soul, just as much as I ever did, and this isn't going to work for me. I have to think of a way out, to think of how to get him to agree to a divorce. I have to think of how to get out of here, and keep custody of my son. I don't want to take Max away from him. Maybe we can co-parent?

I know how much it will hurt to see him with Max, to see what a good dad he is and not have him next to me, no longer even have this name tie of us being married, but what other choice do I have? I don't have family to go to. All I have is Maria, and she has her own husband and her own problems, not to mention she lives thousands of miles away from Grayson.

I'm hoping that my new job can offer me some type of

stability. I hate that I had to buy new clothes with Grayson's card, but I don't have anything professional enough to wear to this type of position. I managed to get a navy blue pantsuit that fits me like a glove to wear on my first day, and as I stride into the office with a puffy face from crying, I feel better about things for just a spilt second.

It's Meredith that greets me, and I smile at her, pleasantly surprised. She hugs me tight and I'd forgotten how touchy-feely she was. Pretty much the opposite of Grayson, although he was fairly affectionate when we were first dating. He doesn't seem like the type to do it in public, though, or when things weren't serious.

"Sister-in-law," she crowed. "I've missed you." She pouted, sticking out her full lower lip. "I thought you were going to call me so that we could go to brunch."

"Sorry," I mumbled. "We just got caught up."

"Newlyweds, huh?" She raises her eyebrows and I give her a wan smile.

"Exactly," I say dryly, even though that can't be further from the truth. The only newlywed thing we'd done is have sex, and that hasn't exactly been lovemaking. And it's never going to happen again.

"Let me show you to your office."

It's small, the office, but it's mine, and it's on the corner so that I can see out over the city. There's a desk over by the wall and a nice, cushiony chair.

"It's lovely," I say honestly.

Meredith scoffs. "It's the smallest office we have, don't humor me."

"I'm not! I've never had an office before," I admit.

Meredith blinks. "Really? The way you aced the tests in the interview, I thought you had plenty of experience."

I flush. "I only worked as a receptionist, but I have a degree in Marketing."

Meredith smiles. "Well, experienced or not, you've got the job and I know you'll do it well. In a bit, I'll introduce you to everyone in the office." She looks down at her watch. "Although they won't be in for another hour or so. Perpetually late," she groans.

I laugh. "I guess big-time executives don't have to be on time."

"They should be," she drawls, and steps out of the office. I get settled in, putting down my briefcase with my laptop in it and looking at the PC on the desk. It's much nicer than my laptop, with programs that I don't have.

Grayson might be right that I need to buy a newer one. I hate to have to use his money for it, but until I get my first paycheck, that's how things have to be. I tell myself one day I'll pay him back for what he's bought for me, if not for Max, but I don't know how I ever will, even with this salary, which is much higher than I anticipated.

I feel terrible today, and it's probably from all the drinking I've been doing, but my stomach definitely feels off. I don't feel hungry at all, and I'm blaming it on the hangovers this weekend and nerves from starting a new job.

A man knocks on my open doorjamb, popping his head into my office.

He's strikingly handsome, blond where Grayson is dark, with bright green eyes. He's tall and broad, and dressed in a fancy three-piece-suit.

"Hello," he says in a low, rumbling voice, and if I wasn't so attracted to Grayson and wrapped up in that, I might have been swooning.

"Hello," I say nervously, having no idea who this man is. "I'm Lillian Whitlock."

His blond eyebrows raise. "Whitlock? I know that Grayson doesn't have any other sisters."

I chuckle. "I'm his wife," I say, and boy, is that weird to say out loud to a stranger.

He grunts in response. "Wife?" The man chokes and clears his throat to cover it. "I had no idea he'd gotten married. Can't believe I wasn't invited."

"And you are?" I ask, curious.

He just stares at me. For such a handsome man, he's kind of lacking in social graces. "I'm Derek Ledderman. I work alongside Grayson in the other building, with the partners."

He gives me a smile that's actually quite charming, despite his demeanor, and I can't help but smile back.

"Are you and Grayson friends?" I ask.

Derek snorts. "I wouldn't say that. Not anymore. We were friends when we were younger, and I still hang around with Lox, but Grayson and I don't exactly see eye to eye when it comes to business."

I nod slowly, as if I understand, but Grayson had never so much as mentioned Derek, when he talks about Loxton regularly. I wonder what it was that made them have a falling out, but I suppose it's none of my business.

"It's nice to meet you, Derek," I tell him, and I mean it. I definitely need new friends and he seems like a nice enough man.

"Nice to meet you, too, Mrs. Whitlock," he says politely. "Let me know if you need anything around the office."

He seems kind, if not a little emotionally stunted. I hum and go back to my work, wondering idly about what might have happened between him and Grayson in the past.

The next couple of hours go by quickly, with the office manager giving me a short tour around the office, and then a pair of heels clicking down the hallway gets my attention when I'm back at my desk.

She opens my door without knocking.

Mallory Whitlock is in my office, and she looks like she means business.

"What are you doing here?" I hiss.

"Thought I'd bring lunch by to my daughter-in-law," she says innocently, plopping down a bag on my desk. When I look inside it's a garden salad, which I hate.

"Thanks," I say dryly, sliding it to one side of my desk. If it doesn't have a ton of meat in it, I don't want it.

"I figured you needed to watch your figure," she says snidely. "That wedding dress fit you pretty snugly."

Mallory shuts the door behind her.

"What do you want, Mallory?" I ask, pinching the bridge of my nose between my index and middle finger. I have a headache on top of a sour stomach, and I'm not in the mood for this.

"I wanted to know what your plan is," she says, sitting down in the chair across from the desk.

"My plan?"

"With Grayson. Do you plan to take off again?" she asks, looking at her perfectly manicured nails.

"I got talked into taking off the first time," I say through gritted teeth. "I wonder who had something to do with that."

"Oh, come *on*, Lillian. You know as well as I do that you had one foot out the door. You and Grayson were never... *are* never going to work out."

"How do you know that?" I demand to know. "What do you even know about me?"

"I know where you come from," she says, raising her chin as if she is any better than me because she had a golden spoon and I didn't.

I scoff. "I don't want to do this with you right now, Mallory." *Or ever.*

"So, you plan to stay with him?"

"That's none of your business."

"That's every *bit* of my business. He's my only son, and I won't have you breaking his heart all over again."

I stand up, slamming my hands down on the desk. "Who broke his heart, Mallory? Who was it that told me I'd never be enough for him? Who broke me down over a series of hours and telling me what a worthless piece of shit I was?"

"You listened," she hisses, also standing. "You know what you are and you know what he is, and it's never going to work."

My hands are shaking. It's not like I can hit her but suddenly I'm trembling all over, feeling nauseous, and instead of responding I burst out of the office and head to the bathroom, barely making it to a stall before I start to throw up.

I should have never taken those tequila shots with Maria.

25

———

GRAYSON

My personal assistant, Marguerite, watches me with her dark eyes as I pace around my office.

"You want to go check on her, don't you? See how she's doing in that other building?"

"Shut up, Marguerite," I grumble.

She laughs. She's only twenty-two, younger than I would have liked for a personal assistant, but she's wonderful at her job, I have to admit. And she knows me too well.

"I just want to know how she's settling in," I say, and Marguerite sighs.

"I could call Meredith and ask her."

I stop pacing. "Would you?"

She nods. "I would. Not like you're going to get any work done until you hear about it."

My shoulders relax and I sit down at my desk. "Thank you."

She gives me a sloppy salute. "Sure thing, boss."

I don't know why I'm so irritated by not knowing how she's settling in, but I think it has a lot to do with the fact that my mother often pops into the office to bring Meredith lunch and I know that she and Lillian had something going on at the wedding. I don't know what it was about, but it didn't seem good.

Not to mention that Derek Ledderman will be working in that office today. I wonder if it isn't a coincidence that he planned his meetings in the conference room there. We had once been best friends, but we had a falling out after Lillian left that I have to admit, was my fault. We should have made up by now, but I can't stand how smug he is about all of it.

Derek, Loxton, and I, though though we don't have the same age, grew up together, all of us from rich back-grounds and running in the same social circles. After Lillian left, I was a mess, and Lox put up with it while Derek didn't, and that's all there is to it. One day, I'll have to handle that and make up with him, but today is not that day.

As I wait for Marguerite to come back with news, I decide that I'm not waiting anymore and head over to the other building myself, where I run almost immediately into Derek.

"Met your wife," he says, and I smirk at him.

"She's gorgeous, right?"

"Hotter than you deserve," he shoots back, but there's no bite to it. Maybe he isn't so bad after all.

I walk past him into Lillian's office, but instead of finding here there, I see my mother, sitting across from her desk.

"What are you doing here, Mother?" I ask her, exasperated.

"Just chatting with your wife," she says. "She looks a little tired, Grayson, you been keeping her up late?"

"That's none of your business," I mutter, and before I can say anything else, Lillian comes back into the room, holding onto the doorjamb.

She *does* look tired. Beautiful in a blue pantsuit, but tired.

"Are you all right, Lillian?" I ask her, steadying her with one hand on her hip as she walks past me to her desk.

"Fine," she says in a garbled voice and then clears her throat. "Just overdid it this weekend."

She gives me a wan smile and I take it she doesn't want my help.

I take in a deep breath. "Has anyone given you a tour? You won't have much to work on today," I tell her.

"Mallory was kind enough to buy me lunch, but I don't think it agrees with me," she says.

"You didn't even try it," my mother mutters, but Lillian ignores her.

"Do we get lunch on this tour?"

I nod. "There's a café down the street we can go to."

She takes my arm, turning around to look at my mother almost smugly. What is going on with them?

"Is there something you want to tell me about you and my mother?" I ask her as we walk through the offices with her arm on my bicep.

"Nope," she says easily. "It's so kind of her to buy me lunch, but she doesn't know I don't like salad."

I snort. "You hate salad."

"Exactly," she answers, humming a little and with more spring in her step than before.

I give her a look, having no idea what's going on but I like her better mood, instead of her crying right after we had sex.

"You're feeling better today?" I ask.

"I'm feeling fine; what do you mean?" She looks up at me innocently.

I guess this is how she's going to play it, like it never

happened. Like she didn't tell me that she still wanted me, that she wanted our marriage to be real.

I clear my throat, annoyed. "Do you just want to get lunch instead of taking a tour?"

"Yes, please," she groans. "I'm starving."

AN HOUR LATER, she's digging into the bacon home fries like they contain the secrets of the universe.

"You gonna take a breath at some point?" I tease.

Lillian grins at me . "I don't know, I might just dive in and live there."

"I can't believe my mother brought you a salad." I chuckle.

Her face sours and she stabs at her fries. "I don't want to talk about your mother."

I lean forward. "Why not? Did you meet her... before?"

Lillian freezes. "I just said I don't want to talk about it, Grayson. Drop it."

I frown but I know that when she gets like this, there's no talking to her. "Fine. How's work going?"

"Kind of boring so far, honestly," she admits, and I laugh.

"It's your first day. Slow down, Killer."

She smiles at me. "I'm just excited."

"You were always smarter than me when it came to marketing, so I'm sure you'll do fine," I say, and I'm telling the truth. She always seemed to know more than I did about my own job, and she was a brilliant marketing executive in between her other jobs that she worked, paying her way through college.

I admire Lilian's resolve, even though if she had told

me about Max she wouldn't have had to work so hard all those years. What was she doing all that time that she was away? Was she with someone else? Did she leave me for someone else? These are the thoughts that keep me up at night.

I sit back against the booth and look at her for a long moment. Fuck it. There's no time like the present.

"Why did you leave?"

Lillian puts her fork down and it clangs on the plate.

"Wh-what?" she stutters.

"Was there someone else? Did you leave me for some other guy?" I ask, gritting my teeth.

"Grayson," she starts, but then closes her mouth.

"No, Lillian, I want to know. You say that you want me back, that you want all of this to be real. You say that you still want me, but how can I believe that when you won't even tell me why you left in the first place?"

"There was no one else," she says quietly, and I search her face for any signs of deception. I don't find any, but then again, I never did. She's always been closed off with her emotions and I don't know how to read her. It drives me crazy.

"How can I be sure of that?" I ask, looking at her almost desperately.

She looks up at me with brown eyes so dark they almost look black.

"Because since I met you, Grayson Whitlock, there's never been anyone else."

"Do you mean that?" I ask hoarsely.

"I mean it," she says firmly, and I believe her.

I swallow hard, not knowing if I want to reveal anything else to her. I know that I'm saying too much, that I'm getting too close to saying what I really mean.

"There's never been anyone else since you for me, either."

Lillian's mouth drops open. "You're not serious. Not in five years?"

I shake my head. "Couldn't bring myself to do it."

"Why?" she asks.

Because no one else measured up is the truth, but that's not what I say.

"Because I never wanted to get hurt like that again."

As soon as I say it, I regret it, because Lillian's eyes shutter as if she's pulled down a blind over her features. She closes up and she feels further away from me than she had when she was really gone.

"I didn't do it to hurt you, Grayson. Please believe that."

For some reason, I do. I don't think Lillian would hurt anyone on purpose. But it doesn't matter. We're still just as far away as we were five years ago when she left.

26

LILLIAN

Work goes by quickly after Grayson drops me off. We're quiet on the walk back to the building and I know that I've probably fucked things up, but what am I supposed to say? Am I supposed to hurt him even more with the truth?

The truth is it doesn't matter anyway. I still left, after all, even though I loved him. I could have come back at any time. Told him about Max. But I didn't do that, either.

On my way home from work, I stop by to pick up a box of crackers and some ginger ale for my stomach, and as I walk past the feminine products aisle I stare at the tampons for a long, long moment.

How long has it been since my period had come? Days? Weeks? I hadn't kept up with it at all since Grayson and I had got married—since the first time we'd had sex since he found me.

Fuck.

I pick up a pregnancy test with shaking hands and take it to the counter, wracking my brain to see if I can remember my symptoms when I found out I was pregnant with Max. It was mostly just that I was *hungry*, all the time, but I'm kind of a big eater anyway, so it's hard to tell. I certainly wasn't this nauseous when I was pregnant with Max, but one thing I know is that every pregnancy is different.

What am I going to do if I am pregnant? If I tell Grayson, he'll never agree to a divorce. He'll tell me that we can do this, that we can continue to be together and "keep up appearances." He still won't forgive me.

I take the test back at home and leave it on the top of the toilet, walking into my room to plop down on the bed and setting an alarm on my phone for five minutes. I'm exhausted all the time, but I thought that was from drinking all weekend.

It's fine. I'm not going to be pregnant. That would be too much, right? No one gets pregnant in an arranged marriage, and Grayson and I had only been together a handful of times.

When the alarm goes off I swallow hard and go into the bathroom, looking down at the test.

Positive.

It's there, in big pink letters, and this is the most expensive pregnancy test they had, so I don't think it's faulty.

I'm pregnant. What am I supposed to do now?

The first thing I do is get back on my bed, lying down face-down, and text Maria.

I'm pregnant.

Instead of texting me back, she calls and I pick up with a groan. Grayson is working late so I don't have to worry about him walking in, and Max is already down to sleep, but still, I hiss into the phone when I answer.

"You're *pregnant!*" she screeches. "Isn't that wonderful?"

I blink. "What do you mean, wonderful? *How* is this wonderful, Maria? Grayson hates me."

She snorts. "That man doesn't hate you. He's so crazy in love with you he can't see straight, but he doesn't hate you."

"What? Where do you get that from?" My heart is racing, and if she were here, I would hit her right in the arm.

"I saw the way he looks at you. The way he took care of you at that bar, stopped the guy that was talking to you. He's crazy about you, Lillian, didn't you know?"

"No, I most certainly don't know, and you're wrong," I say firmly.

"I'm not wrong, but if you don't want to be pregnant, there's ways around that."

My breath catches in my throat. "I don't want that. I want this baby. It's mine." I put my hand to my stomach.

"How are you going to tell him? Are you going to make him dinner or gift him the pregnancy test or something?" Maria asks excitedly.

"Absolutely not! I can't tell him, Maria, what are you, crazy?"

"Yes, it's absolutely crazy for me to tell you to tell your husband and the father of your child that you're pregnant. Sure. I'm the crazy one."

"Listen, Maria, if I have to move in with you, would you be able to take me and Max in?"

"Lillian, you're being ridiculous... Of course you and Max can stay here any time you want, but I don't think you've thought this through."

I take in a deep breath. "You're right. I haven't. I just found out today, so I really haven't had time to think it through."

Moving across country wouldn't work. Grayson had found me there, and he'd find me again. And I don't want to take Max away from him. Max loves his father. God, what am I going to do?

"Take some time and think about it, Lil. Give yourself some space."

I nod and then realize she can't see me. "Okay. Okay, I'll do that."

"Call me back tomorrow, okay? Promise me."

"I promise," I say, but my mind is somewhere else and when she hangs up, I'm a little startled.

I turn over and look up at the ceiling, biting my lower lip so hard that I'm tasting iron in my mouth. I have no earthly idea what I'm going to do, but I know I cannot raise this child in a loveless marriage. It's bad enough that I allow Max to grow up like this.

I have time, I tell myself. *I have at least four months.*

Four months is enough time to save money. It's enough time to figure out what I want to do, maybe convince Grayson we need to get a divorce.

My head is spinning and I throw up again before heading into Max's room, sitting next to his bed and watching him sleep. I could have not had Max, but he's the best thing in my life, and I want to have this baby, I know that much.

I must fall asleep while I'm thinking and watching Max sleep, because the next thing I know, someone is knocking on the doorjamb.

"Lillian? You sleeping in here with Max?" Grayson asks.

I startle awake, rubbing my face. "No, was just watching him sleep."

Grayson enters the room and sits down on the edge of the bed. "I do that too, sometimes. I think about how I've missed so much of his life..." he trails off.

I swallow hard. "I know that's my fault, but Grayson..."

He holds up a hand. "It doesn't matter. When it comes to

Max, whatever happened between me and you doesn't matter. He never has to know any of it."

I nod, agreeing. I don't want Max to know what went wrong between Grayson and me.

"What about us, Grayson? When will it ever not matter between us?"

"I don't know," he says, looking over at me briefly before looking back at Max, brushing his hair back from his face. "I don't know if I can ever let it go, Lillian."

That means that if I do it again, if I leave with another one of his babies in my belly, he'll never forgive me, but I'd already known that. If I make this decision without him, I can kiss any future relationship with Grayson Whitlock goodbye, even the one that's just for appearances.

I stand up and Grayson watches me walk out of the room. He doesn't stop me.

27

GRAYSON

I try to tell myself that I'm not falling in love with her all over again. I try to tell myself that this is just the sex, it's just the nearness and intimacy of being close to another person, and it could be anybody. It doesn't have to be Lillian.

But I've tried being with other women, and it doesn't work. I can't even get my dick to work unless it's with her, for god's sake, and what does that say about me? What kind of billionaire playboy am I?

Before Lillian, women were a dime a dozen. I had a fling or two in college and several one night stands, but those women were just filler. They were my attempts to filling up some kind of void in me, something I didn't even know existed until I met Lillian.

Lillian fills that void like no one else. It's almost like she makes me whole, and it disgusts me. It disgusts me because I shouldn't feel this way. I shouldn't care about her at all, even if she's the mother of my child.

She *left* me. She broke me. And now here I am, worrying myself to death because of how cryptic she'd sounded when she asked me if I could ever forgive her.

What does that mean? Is she thinking of running off again, because if she is, she has another thing coming. If I have to tie her to the bed, I won't allow her to leave me again.

There I go again: leave *me*. Not leave Max, not leave this sham of a marriage, but leave *me*. That's what I'm worried about. That's what hurts the most, is the fact that she might leave me again. *Fuck.* I'm back in it now, worse than it had ever been, now that she's gone and come back, and I don't know what to do about it.

For one of the few times in my life, I stop thinking and act.

Lillian walks out of Max's room and I wait a moment before I follow her out into the hall.

I grab her around the wrist, not gently but not roughly, and she turns to face me, crossing her arms as I drop her wrist. I stare down at her, not speaking.

"What is it, Grayson? I'm tired," she says, and she does sound tired. Bone-tired, really, and I wonder if she's the type of tired I had been when she'd thrown me away.

"Why did you leave?" I ask again, and she sighs heavily.

"I *told* you—" she starts, but I cut her off.

"You didn't tell me a goddamn thing," I say, and my voice is low and even. My sister used to tell me it was eerie when I got mad, because I went as calm as a cucumber.

"It doesn't matter," she says, and I scoff.

"It damn well matters to me, Lillian. You ripped my *heart* out," I say it firmly, seriously, because it's true and it's damn well time she knows it.

Lillian's face changes, something flashing across her expression like lightning.

"No, I didn't," she says, just as firmly. "You never loved me, not really."

"Don't tell me how I feel," I shoot back, and Lillian tilts her head.

"Feel? Not felt?" she asks softly, and I'm getting lost in her eyes, so I look away, clearing my throat.

"Things are different now," I say, and it's true. They are different. I'm a different person and so is she, but when I touch her, she feels so damn familiar, so damn *right*...

"They're not all that different," she says, her tone still quiet and unsure. "I'm still Lillian."

"A *different* Lillian," I tell her. "Just like I'm a different Grayson."

"It feels the same when we're together," she admits, and my eyes shoot back to her face, not believing that she's revealing so much. She's been so shut down the whole time that she's been back, and it's been infuriating.

"What does that mean?" I ask, setting my jaw.

Lillian looks at me for a moment longer and then averts her gaze, shaking her head. She turns and walks toward the guest bedroom.

"Don't walk away from me," I rasp, my throat suddenly raw. "Don't walk away from me again."

Lillian pauses for only a split second before she disappears into the guest bedroom, and something wounded and fragile inside me seems to break. I slam my fist into the wall, shattering the sheet rock and leaving a hell of a hole that I'll have to find someone to repair, but I don't care. I hit it again, and again, until Max comes to his bedroom door, his bright eyes wide.

"Daddy?" he asks sleepily, and I cradle my bleeding hand to my chest so that he doesn't see, plastering on a smile.

"Sorry, buddy. Just got mad."

"I get mad sometimes, too," he says, smiling at me with

his little, even teeth. "It's okay. Will you read me another story?"

I clear my throat. "Give me just a few minutes, okay, pal? I'll be right back."

Max nods, yawning and stumbling back to his bed, and I figure he'll be sleeping again before I come back into the room but wild horses couldn't keep me away.

This is what is important. My son. The only thing keeping me sane.

I head to the master bathroom, washing off my bleeding knuckles with a hiss, and Lillian appears behind me, having managed to tiptoe her way inside without me noticing.

She tsks in the back of her throat. "What did you do?"

"You did it," I say sullenly, and Lillian shakes her head, smiling a little.

"I'll take the blame for pissing you off, but what did the wall ever do to you?"

"It was there," I reply, and Lillian chuckles and begins to look in the medicine cabinet for antiseptic and bandages. She finds them, each bathrooms stays fully stocked with a first aid kit.

I pull away from her when she touches my arm and she sighs.

"Come on, Grayson. Let me fix you up. It's the least I can do."

I look at her for a moment, searching her face, but she's looking down at my bloodied hand. I realize, slowly, that I'm *afraid* of her. I'm not afraid that she'll physically hurt me, of course. I could pin both her wrists above her head with one hand (and had, a few nights in bed together). I'm afraid that she'll leave again, take Max and disappear just as she did before and it would be hell to lose Max, absolute torture.

What I'm coming to terms with is that the real hell would be losing both of them.

The antiseptic stings but I barely acknowledge it, looking down into her face. She's still not looking at me as she begins to bandage my hand, and I let her.

"Lillian," I call quietly, and her brown eyes seem liquid when she looks up at me.

She opens her mouth, wets her lips with her tongue, and I lean down and kiss her, not hungrily like usual but soft, wet and open.

Her mouth opens like she's been waiting for this kiss her whole life, and she melts against me as I hold my injured hand out. I take hold of the back of her neck, pressing her closer as I explore her mouth, and she whimpers against my lips.

I move my hands to her hips, hefting her onto the sink, and she spreads her thighs eagerly. I regret asking her to buy these little nighties but they drive me less crazy than her ex-boyfriend's T-shirts, or whatever she was wearing before. I still want to make my mark on her, make her mine, but the instinct is weaker.

I press against her, hard in my slacks and she reaches her hand between us to grope me and I hiss against her skin.

"I thought you said we shouldn't do this anymore," I whisper, and she groans.

"When you kiss me like that, it's hard to say no."

I can barely think straight with her hand on my dick but I pull my face away to look at her all the same.

"You can always say no, Lillian," I say, and she scoffs.

"Easy for you to say. I'm not as irresistible as you are."

I snort and place my good hand over hers on my crotch. "Don't you feel what you do to me? One kiss and I'm as hard as diamond."

Lillian licks her lips and it makes me growl in the back of my throat. I take hold of her ass and pull her closer to the edge, wondering if I can angle up inside of her or if I'm too tall. Instead, I pull aside the crotch of her panties, getting down on my knees so that I can bury my face in her sex.

She tastes amazing, like musk and honey and I groan against her before lapping at her clit. She puts her hands in my hair, tugging gently and it makes me jolt my hips forward in pleasure. I want to be inside her, buried to the hilt, but I want to make her come first. I slide one finger inside her entrance and when she gasps and clenches around me, I insert another. I hook them upward just the way she likes and her thighs tremble.

"Grayson," she whispers, and the sound of my name on her lips makes my lower abdomen clench with lust.

I latch around her clit, pumping my fingers in and out of her, and it's only a few moments before she's coming, clenching her thighs around my head so that I can barely breathe. I don't care; I'll learn to breathe through my ears if I get to taste her every night.

I gasp in air when she releases her grip, looking up at her, my face probably shiny from her juices and she leans down to kiss me. As I stand, she fumbles with my belt, trying to get it unbuckled so that we can continue.

"Mommy?" a small voice from the doorway of the bedroom calls, and I groan and step away from her, keeping my body angled away from the doorway so that my erection isn't obvious.

"Max," Lillian gasps, closing her legs and hopping down off the counter and I chuckle, looking down at myself tenting my pants.

"You better get him," I manage, and Lillian giggles and

kisses my cheek, heading toward the doorway to scoop Max up in her arms.

Shit. Perils of having a small child, I suppose. I never did read him that story, so this is probably my fault. I wonder if there's a shower cold enough to help me.

28

LILLIAN

I had told myself that I wouldn't sleep with Grayson again, but when he kissed me like that, I just couldn't help myself. What else am I supposed to do when a man like that takes the back of my neck in his hands, kisses me so softly and thoroughly? There's no way that I can resist.

That's why I'm thinking of getting out of here. I don't know how long I can stay in a loveless marriage when we're still sleeping together, still being intimate enough that I'm falling back in love with him. It isn't fair to my heart, which aches every time he tells me that he can't forgive me.

He keeps asking the reasons that I left, but I can't tell him the truth. It would only hurt him and it wouldn't help him forgive me. Would it?

I wake up the next morning for work, only a little disappointed that Grayson hadn't snuck back into my room to finish what we started in the bathroom. I have to throw up twice after brushing my teeth, but I manage to get it together enough to get dressed and put on some light makeup.

Meredith meets me at my office door, bouncing around

excitedly. "I've got your first assignment," she tells me, and I smile wanly. Meredith raises a dark eyebrow, looking almost eerily like her brother. "Are you okay? You look a little... gray."

I wonder if that's supposed to be a joke, but she doesn't seem like she's laughing, staring at me with concern.

"I'm just not feeling well," I mumble, walking past her and taking the file that she has in her hand. I flip through it and it's for a simple ad, but I'm excited, smiling a bit as I sit down at my desk.

"You weren't feeling well the last time I saw you, either," she says suspiciously, and then her blue eyes widen. "Holy shit," she whispers, shutting my office door. "Are you pregnant?"

I shoot my eyes up to her face and I'm sure I look terrified. "Meredith—" I start, trying to decide how to deflect, but Meredith is jumping up and down and squealing.

"A niece! I just know this one is going to be a girl and I'll be the cool aunt and be there for every milestone," she babbles, and I stand up and reach over the desk to put my hand over her mouth gently.

"Meredith," I say seriously. "I'm trying to keep this from Grayson, just for now. I... I need to decide a fun way to tell him," I lie, slowly dropping my hand from her mouth as she calms.

"I understand," she says, but her blue eyes are sparkling. "I'm just excited."

I give her a weak smile. "Of course. I am too," I say flatly, even though excitement isn't exactly what I'd call what I am.

"I should warn you that Mom is here," Meredith says, and I close my eyes briefly, my heart dropping.

"Wonderful," I mutter.

Meredith bites her lip. "I know that the two of you don't

get along very well, but once she knows about the new baby—"

"Meredith! You can't tell her," I say, my voice sounding panicked even to my own ears. "I don't want Grayson to find out."

Meredith sighs. "I'm not going to tell her, but she'll sniff it out. I don't think she'll tell Grayson if you ask her not to, though."

I groan. "I didn't want *anyone* to know."

"Why not? Is something wrong? Trouble in paradise?" Meredith's voice has a teasing lilt but when I look up at her, her face is serious.

"Of course not," I say quickly. "It's just personal and it's really early, so I want to tell him when it's the right time."

That much is true. I know that I'll eventually have to tell Grayson, as much as I don't want to, but I have a few months before it will become obvious. I still haven't decided what I'm going to do. I can't take Max again, and I can't leave him, so I'm sort of stuck.

My head has been spinning since I realized that I was pregnant, and it's beginning to take its toll on my body. The pregnancy is taking its toll, too, and between the two things, I'm barely able to sleep or eat.

My stomach growls as if it read my thoughts and reminded me.

"Is baby hungry?" Meredith asks cutely, and I want to roll my eyes. She's cute, but sometimes she can be a lot.

"A little. Haven't been able to keep much down," I admit, and that's when Mallory knocks on my door.

I begin flipping through the file again, hoping that I won't get sick while she's watching. I don't want her to have any ammunition against me with Grayson, that's for sure.

Meredith opens the door for me before I can protest,

and Mallory comes in bringing what smells like an entire barbeque restaurant. My stomach growls again. I've always craved meat like crazy.

"I brought you something from the barbeque place down the street," she says to Meredith, ignoring me. "Sorry, Lillian. They didn't have any salads," she says snidely, and I *do* roll my eyes, then, although I keep my head down so that she doesn't see.

"I'll share with you, Lil," Meredith says, sitting down on the other side of the desk to spread out the food.

Mallory frowns but doesn't reply, and I can't help myself from beginning to eat as soon as Meredith opens the to-go boxes.

"You certainly are hungry today," Mallory comments, and Meredith clears her throat.

"I think I need a trip to the little girl's room," Meredith says, and I give her a pained look, trying to telepathically ask her not to leave me. She mouths, "I'm sorry," before leaving the room quickly, the tap of her heels audible on the tile floor as she walks down the hallway.

"Are you eating for two, Lillian?" Mallory asks as I sit back in my chair, and I can feel my face go pale.

"I don't know what you're talking about."

"Is it even Grayson's?"

I look over at the door and see Meredith has shut it behind her so that I can speak freely.

"You have a lot of nerve asking me that."

"Do I?" she raises a groomed eyebrow. "Last I checked, you were just a poor girl trying to get all his money."

Anger rises in me like a flood. "If I wanted his money I wouldn't have signed the pre-nuptial agreement, would I?"

"You've got your ways," she drawls. "So, you *are* pregnant, then?"

"I never said that."

"You didn't say you weren't."

I close my eyes, suddenly exhausted. "Mallory, why do you keep doing this? Grayson and I are married. No more damage can be done."

"Divorce is an ugly thing," Mallory says, "but sometimes it's necessary."

I rub at my temples, feeling a headache begin behind my eyes.

"Why do you hate me so much?" I ask tiredly.

"Because you're not good enough for my son," she says simply.

I look up at her. "Is anyone?"

Mallory sets her mouth in a hard line, her lips going thin, but she doesn't respond.

"What, you want him to date some socialite? Paris Hilton?"

"At least she wouldn't be a gold-digger," Mallory snaps.

"I have no idea where you even *get* that. Just because I grew up poor doesn't mean—"

"You're using his money, aren't you? I saw you the other day, shopping with his card. He got you this job. What have you ever done to him except for leave him with his baby in your belly?"

My jaw tightens. "You don't know what you're talking about."

"Don't I? Who do you think had to pick up the pieces? I'm his mother."

"And whose fault is that?" I ask through gritted teeth.

Mallory slams her hands down on the desk and it makes me jump.

"Let's get one thing straight, Lillian. You chose to leave of your own will. Don't try blaming my son's heartbreak on me."

Heartbreak seems like a strong word to me, especially since I didn't even know if Grayson and I had been exclusive at the time that we were dating. For all I knew, he could have had another girlfriend at that time. We hadn't seen each other very long, but it had been long enough for me to fall in love. I don't think he felt the same way, though, no matter what he says. It seems to me that he was just upset that I left him. How dare a poor, plain girl from the wrong side of the tracks leave Grayson Whitlock? It's ego and nothing more. Besides, even if he *had* feelings for me then, he doesn't now.

Which is why this baby is a problem.

"You're right," I say, and Mallory's eyes widen in surprise at my words. "I left. But I came back. So now you're going to have to deal with it. And you won't say a word about my pregnancy to Grayson."

"Like hell I won't," she growls, her palms still on my desk, and I just sit back in my desk chair and smile.

"You won't. Because if you do, the first thing I'm going to do is tell your baby boy the role you played in me leaving."

"You wouldn't," Mallory hisses.

"Try me."

Mallory stares at me for a long moment, as if waiting for me to break, but I stare her down. Finally, she scoffs and jerks open the door, storming outside.

I grin to myself and continue eating the barbeque that Meredith gave me, feeling victorious in a small way.

As I start drawing out some ad plans, Derek calls my name. I remember him from meeting him yesterday. He's handsome enough to have made an impression, plus the awkward way he'd greeted me.

"Yes?" I ask, and he hands me a file.

"I know that they put you on a small ad, but I think you can handle a bigger one. This one's for Breckwood Industries."

"Breckwood? Isn't that—"

"Loxton's family, yes. They deal mostly in textiles—clothing, furniture, you know."

"Yes, I'm aware what textiles are," I say dryly, and Derek blushes just slightly.

"Very well. Anyway, you'll see they need a full commercial instead of the magazine ad that the higher ups gave you. We can work on it together, if you like."

He seems nervous so I smile at him, getting a smile back in return that makes him look more boyish, less grumpy.

"I think that would be nice," I say, and take the file to slide onto my desk. Derek walks out without a goodbye, and I chuckle a little.

Despite Mallory, I like my job, and I even like Derek, a little. I wonder why he and Grayson don't get along.

29

GRAYSON

Maybe Lillian is right. Maybe we *should* stop sleeping together, because all I can do now is think about her. I wanted to sneak into her room later that night when Max was sleeping, but I restrained myself. She told me that I was hard to resist but she's the one who walks around the house in those little nighties and a pair of panties. I think about her long legs, the way she wrapped them around me, while I'm at work and I groan, hardening under my desk.

She's just a building over, and I'm thinking about going to visit her office so that I can see if she's interested in a little afternoon delight. It's well after lunch, and I haven't taken a break so I get up from my desk, adjusting myself in my slacks.

As I head over to the building, I see my mother's car in the parking lot.

"Shit," I mutter, walking faster. I know that my mother and Lillian don't get along, although I don't understand why. They barely know each other, after all, but my mother has always been protective, so I figure it's that.

As I walk through the doors, I can see Lillian's office and

Derek Ledderman is standing in the doorway, speaking to her. I see Lillian smile at him and I frown. I know of course that they work together, but I'd made sure that Lillian had a project that didn't include him. It isn't like I don't trust him with her—he's not a playboy like Loxton by anyone's standards, but what reason does he have to talk to her?

Meredith meets me in the hall and I roll my eyes.

"Don't you have work to do?" I ask, and Meredith rolls her eyes right back.

"I'm working on a project with your wife, but it's such a small one. Why won't you ever let me in on the big projects?"

"Because you're a baby," I say flatly, and Meredith groans and stomps her foot, proving my point.

"I'm *not* a baby. Daddy didn't give me this job because he thought I would screw it up."

"*Daddy* gave you this job because you're his baby girl, and that's that," I say, and Meredith sighs heavily.

"You don't know what you're talking about," she mutters, and I'm looking over her head to see that Derek is *still* in Lillian's office.

"What's Derek doing in there?" I frown.

"Hitting on your wife," Meredith says, and then giggles. Knowing Derek, that would be a near-impossible thing for him to be doing, but still, the idea of it rankles me.

"You're hilarious," I grumble, and finally walk around her. By the time I get to Lillian's office, Derek is gone and Lillian's alone, so I walk inside and shut the door and the blinds.

Lillian stares at me. "What are you doing?"

I shrug. "Checking in on you," I tell her.

She narrows her eyes. "Why are you checking in on me? I didn't get this job because I'm your wife, you know?"

"It certainly didn't hurt," I shoot back, and she frowns at me.

"Don't be a jerk, Grayson. I've got work to do."

"I'm being a jerk because I've got blue balls," I grumble under my breath, and Lillian raises an eyebrow.

"What was that?"

"Nothing," I say brightly. "Have you had lunch?"

"Barbeque. Your mother brought it." The way she says "mother" sounds like she means "bitch," but I don't respond to that.

"I was going to take you out to lunch."

"I didn't know that," she replies, going back to her work.

I lean over the desk. "Lillian."

She looks up at me inquisitively. "Grayson."

"I want to finish what we started last night," I murmur, and her cheeks flush red.

"What do you mean?" she asks innocently, and I groan.

"You know what I mean."

Lillian gives me a slow half-smile. "We can't do it *here*," she says, looking around.

"Seems like there's plenty of space. Worried you can't be quiet, Mrs. Whitlock?"

She bites her lip. "I don't think *you* can be quiet."

"Try me," I say, and she stands up and I begin to grin.

"Sit down on the couch," she orders, and I raise an eyebrow at her tone.

"This is a role reversal, you telling me what to do."

"Don't like it, you can leave," she says, and I sigh and sit down heavily on the couch, spreading my legs and resting my back against the cushion.

Lillian is wearing a navy blue skirt that goes down to the tops of her knees and fits her like a glove, and I lick my lips as she walks around the desk toward me.

She spreads her thighs and walks forward, one heel on either side of my legs and I reach up to grab her around the waist, picking her up and depositing her on my lap.

She squeaks. "I thought you were going to let me tell you what to do."

I snort. "If you thought that, you must not know me very well," I murmur, sliding my hands up her hips to bunch her skirt up.

She spreads her thighs, her knees on either side of me, as I rock her back and forth against my hard length.

She gasps. "You're hard already?"

"I'm always hard for you," I say honestly, but lust flashes across her features. She licks her lips again and leans down to kiss my throat.

I moan low and quiet in the back of my throat, thrusting up against her. Something keeps niggling at me so I can't help but ask.

"What was Derek doing in here?"

Lillian pauses rolling her hips. "Why do you ask? We work together."

"You're not working on a project together," I say, and she looks at me with her head tilted.

"How do you know that?"

"You don't think I have a say in which projects my employees get?"

"I'm not just your employee."

"Exactly," I reply, sliding my hands along the sides of her breasts, wanting to rip the buttoned blouse off of her but restraining myself.

"We *are* working on a project together. He offered me a big commercial."

I frown. "Did he now?"

"Don't be jealous, hubby," she says in a teasing lilt, and my hips thrust up almost automatically at the pet name.

"Who says I'm jealous?"

"The way you grit your teeth when you talk about it. Derek doesn't seem even remotely interested in me, so don't worry."

"He's not interested in any woman," I comment.

"Then why are you jealous?"

"I'm *not* jealous," I mutter. "There's just too many men in this office."

"I've only met Derek. No one's given me a tour yet," she comments. "Maybe there are more handsome men than Derek who want to work with me."

I growl, "Don't you dare."

"Don't I dare what?" She rolls her hips against me, driving me crazy. I pant against her throat before kissing her there and then biting down at the base of her throat.

She moans and then smacks me on the shoulder. "Grayson! I'll have a hickey."

"So? Everyone knows I'm your husband." I reach down to undo my belt and button with one hand, groaning as I release myself.

Lillian looks down at my length with her mouth open, and I catch it with my own, rocking her against me again with only a little piece of fabric between us.

When I pull away, I tug up her skirt, looking around at her ass. "Are you wearing a thong?"

"Helps with panty lines," she replies, blushing a little.

"Fuck," I curse, my mouth going dry. I can't think of anything else but being inside her, so I reach up under the cursed skirt and rip the panties off at one side.

Lillian makes a sound of disapproval that turns into a long moan when I guide myself into her. She seats herself on me like a champ, taking me to the hilt, and my brain seems to shut off as I give small thrusts to get her used to me.

"Jesus, you're tight," I manage, taking her ass in my hands so that I can bounce her on top of me.

Lillian's rolling her hips, mouth open again, and I attack her throat with kisses and bites over and over, uncaring if I left marks. I want this whole damn office to know that she's mine.

It's only a few thrusts before I'm close, gritting my teeth to keep from coming before she does, but she's moving back and forth, her hands on my shoulders, head thrown back, and I know she's close by the way she's pulsing around me.

"Grayson, fuck," she whispers, trying to stay quiet, and I wrap my hand around her throat to get her to look at me.

She gasps, looking right into my eyes, and that's all it takes for me to come. Shit.

It doesn't seem to matter to Lillian that I've already arrived, though, she continues rolling her hips as I hiss from the overstimulation, using me to get off as she stutters out a long moan, clenching around me.

"Fuck me, that's hot," I tell her, looking at her with awe, my hand still around her throat, squeezing slightly.

"Choke me harder," she orders, and I squeeze tighter. Her eyes roll back in her head when she comes and I choke on air because it feels good even though I've already come.

I loosen my grip dand she collapses against me, breathing hard.

She goes limp and I frown, stroking her hair. "Are you okay?"

"Just a little dizzy," she mumbles, and I push her away to look at her face. She looks pale and tired.

"What's going on with you? Are you sick?" I ask, and something like panic flashes in her eyes.

"I haven't been feeling well," she admits, and I frown.

"You should have told me."

"It's not contagious, I don't think," she says, brushing her hair back from her face, and I roll my eyes.

"I don't care if it's contagious, Lillian, I just feel bad fucking you within an inch of your life when you're sick."

Lillian smirks. "You think that was within an inch of my life?"

I growl, "Don't taunt me while you're sick."

She sighs. "I'm sorry I didn't tell you. It's nothing, probably just a summer cold from the change in climate."

I looked at her suspiciously. I guess she's right, the change in temperature from New York to balmy California is quite large.

Lillian steps off me, her legs shaky and I steady her with a hand on her hip before tucking myself back into my pants.

She goes back to her desk and her panties slide down one of her legs since I ripped them. I can't help but laugh, standing to grab her ankle and slide them off. She stares at me as I press them to my face, breathing her in, and then put them in my pocket.

"Hope you have fun on your project with Derek," I say, buttoning my pants and buckling my belt and walking out of the office, leaving her door wide open.

30

LILLIAN

I don't see Grayson much for the next few days. He's working on a big project, and so am I, working closely with both Meredith and Derek. Grayson's avoiding the question of what happened with him and Derek, and it bugs me. What if it was a woman? What if Grayson had been lying to me when he said he wasn't with anyone else?

I get home before he does on the third day, and Max is having a sleepover with one of his friends so they're playing in his room. I check on them and take them some snacks—pepperoni and cheese, Max's favorite, before going to lie down on the couch.

I must have dozed off, because the next thing I know Grayson stumbles through the doorway, dropping his keys.

"Fuck me," he curses, leaning over to pick them up, and I sit up on the couch, my eyes wide.

"What are you doing home so late?" I ask suspiciously, looking at my watch. It's after nine.

"Business dinner," he mutters, and I frown. The last time he had a business dinner he came home smelling like women's perfume. I resist the urge to go and sniff him.

He braces his hand against the couch.

"Are you drunk?" I ask, and Grayson gives me a big grin.

"Maybe," he comments, plopping down on the couch next to me.

He leans his head against my shoulder.

"Too many drinks at the business dinner?" I ask, and Grayson nods.

"I swear, some of these clients can drink like fishes," he mutters, "and too much champagne gives me such a headache, sometimes."

I rub his temples with my fingers and he groans. "That feels nice."

I hum, still rubbing, my heart racing just a bit at being this close to him. This seems very domestic, like we're actually married for real instead of just for show, and it makes me nervous.

"Max is having fun with Clay," I tell him, and Grayson grunts in response, like he's half-asleep. I can hear the boys giggling from the other room. "I have to admit I let him stay up late. Fell asleep on the couch."

Grayson had closed his eyes and now he opens them, frowning a little. "Are you still feeling sick?"

I shrug. "Only a little."

Grayson sits up a bit. "I'll get Max into bed. He can go without a bath for tonight, since he has a friend over."

"You've got a headache," I complain, and Grayson snorts.

"It's my own fault, so I should suffer."

I laugh at that and he stands up albeit unsteadily but straightens out as he heads down the hallway.

I yawn, still tired, and shift on the couch and lie down. I have to admit that it's good that he's doing something else. I don't think my heart can take him being so sweet and vulnerable. I doze off for a bit and when I wake up, it seems extra dark. When I look at my watch again, I realize it's nearly midnight, so I get up with a grimace and walk toward Max's room.

Grayson is sprawled out on Max's double bed with the boys cuddled around him. He's snoring softly, and Max is too, almost in the same tone. My heart aches. Is this what it would be like to have two kids? Grayson is a good father to Max, wouldn't he be just as good to another child?

I slowly close the door and head back to my bedroom. I have a lot to think about. I'm sure that Mallory would be overjoyed if I asked for a divorce, but I don't know how Grayson would take it. Would he even let me see Max?

Panic rises in my throat when I think about leaving my baby boy, and I know that I can't do it, not for long, anyway. Is there a way I could leave just long enough to have the baby? Give it up for adoption? I don't know if I can do that, either, not after having Max and loving him so much, but maybe that's what's right. I don't want the kids to grow up in this complicated relationship. Once they're older, they'll start noticing that Mommy and Daddy never touch each other outside of private, that we don't look at each other the way other parents do.

I don't want it to negatively affect them.

I suddenly have to throw up again before bed, and this time I barely make it to the bathroom. As I retch, there's a knock on the bathroom door.

Shit. Grayson.

"Don't come in!" I warn.

"You're sick. Let me help you," he tells me, and then I hear a click in the door and he opens it.

I groan, holding my hair back as I lean over the toilet. Grayson settles behind me, one arm going around me, the other holding my hair.

My face is aflame. "Grayson, get out of here. It's gross."

"In sickness and in health, right?" he murmurs, and my heart skips a beat... just before I throw up again. He starts to rub my back in small circles as I gasp for air and flush the toilet, and it does seem to help.

"You don't have to do this," I say, but I lean against him and he strokes my hair.

"I know," he responds, but he doesn't move until I start to doze off against his chest.

Before I know it, he's picked me up and is carrying me toward the bed, bridal style.

I murmur, tucking my head in against his chest, and when he lies me down on the bed I whimper,

"Don't go. Just hold me a little while. Please?" I plead, feeling dizzy and nauseous.

Grayson looks down at me and there's something on his face that I can't name, but he crawls into bed with me, loosely draping his arm around my waist.

I snuggle back against him, sighing happily.

"Just until I fall asleep," I murmur, and Grayson kisses my temple. It's so sweet that it makes tears spring to the backs of my eyes. He's just being nice because I'm sick, but it means so much to me.

"Just until you fall asleep," he agrees. He usually leaves right after sex, and since I came back, he's never held me like this without any sex.

It's easy to fall asleep in his arms, but I know his side of the bed will be cold and empty when I wake.

I wake up in a few hours, getting sick again, and Grayson's still there, snoring softly. As I bolt out of bed, he knocks on the door again.

"I'll just pick the lock, Lillian," he says, and I groan and open the door, still hunched over the toilet.

"You're going to the doctor," he says firmly, and I shake my head.

"I just need to rest," I say.

"Then you're calling in to work today," he replies, helping me up. I brush my teeth and spit into the sink, looking over at him.

"I haven't been there long enough to call in," I insist.

"It's not like I'm going to fire you," Grayson says dryly, and I snort out a laugh, leaning my forehead against his chest. He makes those little circles on my back with his hand again and I arch my back. My lower back has been aching and it feels good so I groan.

"Don't make noises like that while you're sick," he murmurs, and I smile, lifting my head to look at him.

"Why are you being so nice to me?"

Grayson shrugs. "You're sick. It'd be a real asshole move to be a jerk to you now."

I hum in the back of my throat and manage to crawl into bed where Grayson pulls up the covers and tucks me under them.

"I'll let work know you're not coming, and I'll tell Holly to look after Max and Clay until Clay's mom picks him up," Grayson says, and then kisses my forehead before walking out, closing the door softly behind him.

I have to leave. I can't deal with the way my heart is swelling at his kindness. I just don't know how to do it.

31

GRAYSON

"Are you going out with us tonight?" Derek asks when I get to work and I clear my throat, surprised.

"You don't usually go out. What's up with you?" I ask suspiciously.

Derek shrugs. "I don't know. Networking. Some of the new guys from the other building are going."

I guess Derek has always cared about networking if nothing else. The big fight we had was silly, really, just butting heads on a project, but I'd just been getting over Lillian and I'd been in a bad mood all the time.

I think about it, and I decide there's no reason to go other than to go home and check on Lillian, and I can always call Holly to do that. I shouldn't want to do it myself, anyway. I'm falling harder and harder and I won't be able to take it if she leaves me again. I also can't forgive her and be with her for real, so it all seems like an exercise in futility.

"Where are we going?"

It turns out to be a bar and grille near the office, and after five I head there, hitching a ride in Derek's car.

"Does this mean you forgive me?" Derek asks dryly.

"Why? You been waiting with baited breath?" I joke, and Derek gives me a look at the red light.

"Yes, Grayson," he says flatly. "I've been losing sleep over it."

I bark out a laugh and clap him on the shoulder. "Sure, I forgive you. Hardly even remember what it was about."

Derek grunts, and that's his sign of approval, so we finish the short ride in comfortable silence.

There's several people from the other building, including Meredith, and somehow Loxton has gotten invited too, even though he's never done a day's work in his life.

"Where's Lillian?" Meredith asks with a pout.

"She's not feeling well," I respond, and Meredith gives me a strange look. "What was that look?"

"Nothing," Meredith says quickly, heading off to the bar to order another one of her fruity cocktails.

I stare after her, but I can't figure out what's going on. Loxton is drunk already, and Derek is sitting there, stone-faced.

"You're a real fun time at parties," I joke, and Derek smiles at me.

"Thank you."

I chuckle and sip my scotch. I've been drinking too much lately, but mostly it's been to get my mind off of Lillian. I think about her all the time, and it's becoming a problem.

"What's her name? Lilith?" someone says, and my ears perk up. I look down toward the end of the pushed together tables that the ten of us are sitting at and see a face I don't recognize.

"Lillian," I say, and the guy groans.

"Lillian. Sexy name," he says, "sexy girl."

"Oh, you think so?" I ask, teeth gritted, and Derek puts a hand on my shoulder.

"I'm too old and not drunk enough to get in a bar fight with you," he warns.

"You are thirty-seven, not exactly a senior citizen, are you? Besides, Lox has my back. He's only just about thirty, and he actually *is* drunk enough," I shoot back, and Derek laughs, shaking his head.

"That ass in those A-line skirts?" the guy continues, whistling. "I can't wait to ask her out."

"Have you asked if she's married?" I ask calmly, anger rushing through me, making my skin feel hot.

"Who cares?" the guy laughs, and his asshole friends laugh along with him.

"Interesting," I say quietly, and Derek is staring at me. I'm also too old and not drunk enough to get in a bar fight, either, but if that asshole keeps talking about my wife that way... .

It turns out his name is Jeffrey, and I keep an eye on him the rest of dinner but he doesn't mention her again. I'm on my fourth scotch when Loxton sidles up next to me.

"Are we taking out this Jeffrey guy, or what?" he asks.

I raise an eyebrow. "Why would you care?"

"He's hit on Meredith like ten times already, man, haven't you been paying attention?" Lox asks.

My smile thins. "Oh, so he's going to hit on my wife *and* my baby sister."

"Right? Only I can do that," Lox jokes, and I roll my eyes.

Loxton is harmless, so I've never had to worry about it.

"You really want to get in a bar fight?" I ask him.

Lox shrugs. "It's not like it'd be the first one."

It has been a long time since we've been in a bar fight,

and I'm at work, but it's not like I can get fired. I'm practically royalty in the family business, after all.

"Hey Jeffrey!" I call, heading over to where he is at the bar.

"Yeah?" His cheeks are flushed red with alcohol, and he seems surprised that I'm talking to him.

"Do you know who I am?" I ask.

He shakes his head. "No. Why, have we met before?"

I shrug. "Maybe. Probably I've seen you around the office."

"Have you been with the Whitlock group for a while?" he asks politely.

I smile but I'm sure it doesn't reach my eyes. "You could say that."

"I'm sorry I don't remember meeting you," he says, and sticks his hand out to shake mine.

I ignore it. "Seems like you've met my wife."

He raises an eyebrow and holds out his hands. "Hey, look, I don't mess around with wives."

"That's not what you said earlier," I growl.

"Who's your wife?" he asks.

"Lillian. Last name Whitlock."

His eyes widen. "Wh-Whitlock?"

I nod. "I'm Grayson Whitlock. Nice to meet you."

I think about how he talked about Lillian's ass and I punch him right in the mouth. It devolves quickly after that, with Lox tackling his friend with a laugh and Derek sighing deeply and pulling me off of Jeffrey, but not before he got in a good right hook that caught me above the eye.

My eye fills with blood as the shallow wound bleeds profusely, and the bartender is yelling for security.

Derek pulls me and Lox out of there before the cops

show up and throws us in his car, having had one drink to my four and Lox's god knows how many.

Lox is giggling in the backseat, holding his stomach. "Oh, fuck, I think I bruised a rib."

"Do I need to take you to the hospital, you maniac?" Derek asks, but we'd been in situations like this before, when we were young.

"Nah, I'll walk it off. I can bandage them up myself," Lox assures him.

We had all been a bunch of rough and tumble teenagers, to say the least.

"What about you, killer?" Derek asks, but I've got a napkin held to my head and the bleeding seems to have finally stopped. I blink the blood out of my eye and shake my head.

"I'm good to go."

"This is what I get for being friends with you again," Derek says flatly, and I choke out a laugh, my head spinning with the booze and the adrenaline from the fight.

Lillian is asleep on the couch again when I return, and I tiptoe toward my room not to wake her.

"Gray?"

I freeze in the hallway, not wanting to turn around. I don't want her to see my injury.

"Yeah?"

"Where have you been?" she asks.

"Out," I answer.

Her footsteps sound behind me and I curse as she walks around me in the hallway, looking up at me.

"What the hell happened to you? Did you take up street fighting in the last few weeks?"

I chuckle. "No. It's your fault again. Everything's your

fault," I find myself saying, my words slightly slurred after four drinks and a punch to the head.

Lillian tsks just like she did when I hurt my knuckles, and she goes to the kitchen to grab a warm rag.

"I think you just like to blame me for everything."

"Some asshole from work was talking about your ass," I say, and Lillian snorts.

"I haven't even met any guys at work. Well, except Derek. He doesn't seem like the type."

"He's not," I respond. "He helped me with the fight, though."

"How many guys did you fight?" she asks, dabbing at the wound while I wince in pain.

"Just one, but he had friends," I respond.

"Maybe you should stick to punching walls," she says, and I'm surprised into a laugh.

"Maybe," I admit, looking down at her. I feel this swell of love for her that's always tinged with pain, always tinged by those years I spent looking for her. "You know, I was crazy in love with you back then."

I don't know what I'm saying. I'm drunk and I've been punched in the face and I shouldn't be saying any of this. I shouldn't even let her patch me up, should have done it myself.

Lillian makes a surprised noise. "No, you weren't."

"You don't know. You left," I shoot back. "And it doesn't matter now, anyway."

"Right, because you can't forgive me," she says flatly.

"Right," I say, feeling angry for no reason I can think of, and she finishes wiping the blood off my face and throws the rag into the laundry basket in the bathroom.

"Of course not. What was I thinking," she mutters.

"I don't need your help," I say, although she's already

helped my wound feel better without all the blood crusting around it. I'm angry and I'm not sure why. I think I'm just angry that we aren't together anymore, and it's her fault. "I can take care of myself."

"Sure you can," she says. "That's why you came in covered in blood. It's all over your shirt, you should change it."

I shrug and rip my shirt off, popping buttons and tossing it on the floor. "Is that better?"

Lillian stares at me for a long moment before coming toward me and jumping up into my arms, kissing me hungrily, our teeth gnashing together.

My arms go around her hips and ass as she clenches her thighs around my waist, and I carry her to my bedroom.

32

LILLIAN

I know that I shouldn't be doing this. I know that I shouldn't be having sex with Grayson *again*, especially after I've made my decision, but it's like I can't help myself. He's covered in blood and he ripped off his shirt and he just looks so *good.*

Grayson carries me to his room, depositing me on the bed and covering my body with his own. He slides down as if he's going to eat me out but I tug at his hair, too impatient.

"I don't need that," I rasp. "I just want you."

Grayson curses. "Eager, aren't you, sweetheart?"

"Yes. I'm always eager for you, Gray," I tell him, unable to lie to him now when I need him inside me. The hormones have made me want him all the more, as if my body knows he's the father of the baby growing inside me.

"Damn right. You're my wife."

He loves to say that when we're having sex, loves to remind me that we're in this marriage. I hate it. It doesn't mean anything because it isn't real. He doesn't love me, even if he did before. He hates me.

Grayson tugs off my shorts and I kick to get them all the way off, just as eager as he accused me of being.

I'm surprised when he flips me over onto my stomach, taking a handful of my ass in his hand.

"This ass is mine," he growls. "All of you is mine."

I gasp in pleasure as he spreads my thighs apart, the sound of him fumbling with his belt almost excruciating.

"Grayson, please—"

"Please what, sweetheart? Use your words," he demands, and I turn my head to look at him even though the angle is awkward.

"Please fuck me," I whisper, not wanting to wake Max up even though the master bedroom is across the hall from Max's room.

"Don't have to ask me twice," Grayson mutters, and slides into me, deeply, my ass bouncing against him as I roll my hips back.

He thrusts in and out of me, slowly and deeply, and I need it harder, faster.

I groan and try to rock my hips back against him, trying to get up on my knees but he won't let me, pinning me down.

"Tell me you're mine," he growls.

"I'm yours, Grayson. I've always been yours." I know this isn't the first time I've said it, but it sounds too real, too true, and I tell myself that after this, I have to do it. I have to ask for a divorce.

Grayson starts to fuck me harder, faster, his hands on my hips for purchase, and I grab hold of the headboard to keep myself from sliding backward, crying out in little gasps.

I'm so close to coming that there's black spots blooming behind my closed eyes, and that's when Grayson grabs my ponytail, wrenching my head around to look at him.

"Look at me when I'm fucking you. Want to see your face when I make you come," he orders, and I swallow, my throat dry.

"I'm coming," I say in a broken whisper. "I'm coming, I'm coming."

My orgasm hits me hard and Grayson drops my hair to fuck me faster. My head falls into the pillow, my moans muffled as he thrusts through my orgasm.

I'm almost on the verge of another when he pulls out, spraying all over my ass and lower back. I think idly that if he'd done that more often, I wouldn't be in the situation I'm in.

I expect him to get up and leave or tell me to leave, but instead he plops down next to me, panting and looking at the ceiling. He reaches over to a pile of clothes on the floor (he's messy the day before the housekeeper comes) and rubs a T-shirt over the mess on my ass. I'm far from clean but it's not uncomfortable, and I'm exhausted now so I just lie there, catching my breath.

"I'll leave when my legs work again," I tell him, and Grayson frowns.

"Who says you have to leave?"

I blink at him. "We usually part ways... after."

Grayson waves a hand dismissively. "That's stupid. You don't have to leave. Sleep here if you like."

I look at him, biting my lip. I should get up. I should go back to my bedroom and lie down, go to sleep and forget all about this.

Instead, I snuggle up next to him, and the next thing I know, I'm drifting off.

When I wake, Grayson's gone, and there's no sign of him. I frown, thinking he's left for work early, but when I sit up and rub my eyes, he comes back into the room, carrying a tray.

"What's this?" I ask.

"You need something in your stomach," he states, as if it's a totally normal thing to cook breakfast for your fake wife.

"Did you make this?" I ask. "I didn't know you could cook."

Grayson rubs the back of his neck sheepishly. "I can't; it's leftovers from Holly making Max breakfast," he admits.

It's mostly sausage and bacon with a few eggs, and I wolf it down hungrily.

This is why I need a divorce, I think to myself. He can't keep doing this, being so kind to me but not loving me, and it's making me nuts.

"If we hadn't gotten married, would you have taken Max from me?" I ask him, and he startles as if he wasn't expecting that question.

He sits on the edge of the bed, clearing his throat. "I don't think so. That was my first instinct, I won't lie. But seeing you with him and how much he loves you... " he trails off.

I nod slowly. "If I had known how good you would be with him... " I trail off, too, not knowing how to say that I shouldn't have left.

Grayson's quiet for a long moment. "Are you ever going to tell me why you left?"

"I'm really sorry, Grayson. I know that's no excuse and what I did can never be forgiven, but I was scared and confused, Grayson," I say, and that's not a lie. I was both of those things when I left.

"You could have told me," he says quietly. "We would have worked it out."

"When I left, I didn't know. You have to believe me. If I had, I don't know if I would have been able to leave. But you're right. As soon as I found out, I should have told you. Unfortunately, it's too late to change things now," I say, and he's quiet. I look at him. "Right?"

My heart races. If he gives me a sign, any sign at all, that we could be in love again, then I won't ask for the divorce. We'll have this baby together.

"It's too late, now," he says, barely audible, and my heart sinks to my toes.

"I think I'll get up and get ready for work," I tell him. "I need to shower."

Grayson nods slowly. "You can use the tub if you like," he tells me, and I flash back to the last time I'd used that tub, when he'd walked in on me.

I shake my head. "No, thank you. I need the spray of hot water." I pause. "Thank you for breakfast."

"You're welcome," he says flatly.

I put the tray down on the nightstand and stand up. I wait for just a moment to see if he'll say anything, and when he doesn't, I find my shorts and pull them on, walking out of the room toward my bedroom. Before I close the door, I pause, ad without looking at him, I add, "I really am sorry, Grayson, for everything." And without waiting for a reply I know won't come, I step outside of his room and close the door.

It's too late. There's nothing I can do to fix this relationship, nothing I can do to make him fall back in love with me again. I walk to my room, holding back the sobs that threaten to wreck me as tears stream silently down my face. Just a few steps more. I just need to hold myself together for a few more steps. In the shower, I can hide my sobs.

33

GRAYSON

Work seems to go by so slowly that I feel like time is going backward. I don't know why; usually I like the distraction, but with Lillian only a building away, it seems like torture. I want to go to her, to try and fix things, but I don't know how.

The only thing I could do is cut off the physical part of our relationship. We keep getting closer and closer. I keep feeling more and more, and I can't do this anymore. I just have to tell her it's over, but I shouldn't do it at work.

I'll wait until I get home, tell her there, where she can't storm off. At least that's what I tell myself, but I can't wait, find myself walking over to her building. Jeffrey ducks and hides when I walk through the doors of the building, and it makes me smirk.

Lillian's door is closed, which makes me frown, but when I knock she calls for me to open it.

She's deep in the midst of some kind of presentation, with large poster boards spread out all around her on the floor. It's nearing the end of the day, so I'm surprised that she's still working so hard.

She has her laptop open, too, and I have to step around it to get into the office.

"What are you doing here?" she asks, irritated, and I bite the insides of my cheeks, thinking maybe this isn't the best time.

"Just wanted to see how you were feeling," I lie, and she tilts her head, arching her back as if it hurts.

"I'm on the mend," she says, but she really doesn't look it. She's still too pale.

"When's your presentation?" I ask.

She looks at her watch. "In about an hour," she says. "It's a big one, the commercial for Breckwood Industries."

"Ah," I say, and I've heard that Whitlock was taking on Loxton's family business as a client, but he didn't seem to care or talk much about it. It makes more sense now that he went to the dinner last night.

"You came here for a reason," Lillian says. "Spit it out, Grayson."

I take a deep breath, letting it out through my nostrils. "I thought I should come and tell you that you were right."

"Right about what?" she asks, looking up at me curiously.

"Everything. You were right when you said that we should stop."

"Stop what?" she asks flatly, although I know she knows what I mean.

"Having sex," I say bluntly, and Lillian's lips tighten and she looks away.

"Sure," she says. "Whatever."

I frown, tilting my head, confused. Why would she be upset about that? She's the one who suggested it in the first place.

"Are you mad?"

"I'm not mad, Grayson," she says tiredly, pinching the bridge of her nose between her index and middle fingers. "Why would I be mad? You're giving me what I want."

"Am I?" I ask softly, looking down at her, but she won't look at me.

"I understand," she says. "You can go, let me finish my presentation."

"I don't want to go if you're angry, Lillian—"

"Just go!" she pleads, and I growl and turn around, walking out of her office.

I'm mad as hell now, and I don't know what to do with it. I know I shouldn't have done this at work, but I had just felt so fucked up about everything. It had seemed like the easiest way, at the time.

I hang around in Lillian's building to see how the presentation goes, and when she and the others come out of the conference room, everyone is smiling, so I assume that it went well.

I try to catch her eye before she goes back into her office but she hurries there, closing the door behind her.

I sigh. I'll have to try and catch her at home.

I head back over to my building and half-ass the rest of my work day, returning home and playing with Max for a couple of hours. We build a Lego pirate ship before it's time for his bath, and he goes right to sleep in my arms as we watch television.

Lillian comes home late, around eight, and I frown as she walks through the door.

"What are you doing home so late?"

"Dinner with Breckwood," she says, sounding exhausted.

"Drinks?" I ask, and she shakes her head.

"I wasn't feeling up to it," she admits.

"You should lie down. I'll carry big boy to bed," I tell her.

Lillian doesn't complain, just nods and wearily goes to her room. I guess I should stay out of there so that I'm not tempted to kiss her, but I'm worried about her.

I shower first, hoping that the cold water will keep my skin from heating up by seeing her. When I knock on her door, she calls for me to open it.

She's sitting up, fully clothed, and there's a bag packed by her bed.

"What the hell is this?" I ask, panic rising in my throat and chest. Is this for some kind of business trip? Wouldn't they have told me?

"I'm going to stay at a hotel for a while," she says quietly. "I got my first paycheck, so you don't have to worry about paying for it."

"I don't give a fuck about the *money*, Lillian, why are you going? Is it because I said we should stop having sex?" I take a few steps closer to her. "If that's what it is, we can continue, I just thought—"

Lillian holds up a hand to stop me. "No. You were right. We need to get a divorce."

It feels like she's dumped a bucket of cold water on my head. "Divorce? What are you *talking* about? We got married for a reason, Lillian—"

She cuts me off. "The wrong reason. Your mother hates me, so she won't care that we're divorcing, and if we co-parent well, we can keep it out of the news for a long time. Long enough that no one will care. Billionaires get divorced all the time, trade in for a new model."

"I don't want a new model," I say quietly, and it feels like between the pain and the anger I might burst apart at the seams.

"You don't want me, either."

I slam my hand against the doorjamb and it booms through the house. "Don't tell me what I fucking want, Lillian."

"Well, then you tell me, Grayson!" she cries, tears streaming down her face. "You want to fuck me but you don't want to love me. You want me here but you don't want me sleeping in your bed after sex... oh, except sometimes, you do. Make up your mind!"

"So, you're going to leave? Leave Max?"

Lillian sighs. "Only for a little while. Just a few days, and then we'll work out some kind of custody agreement."

"You're abandoning your child. Any lawyer could see that," I spit out.

"Are you going to tell the lawyer that I abandoned our child? Would you really do that, Grayson?"

"I don't know; are you really that much of a shitty mother?" I say, and I know it's the wrong thing. I know it's going to kill her to hear that and as her face falls, my anger dissipates and I feel like shit. "Lillian—"

"If Max asks to call me, let him," she says. "I'll answer the phone, but only if you text me beforehand."

"You can't *do* this, Lillian!" I take hold of her bag and throw it on the bed, pulling all the clothes out and putting them back into her drawers, dropping a few as I do it. I'm panicked, unable to think straight. I can't lose her again.

"I can't raise a child in a loveless marriage, Grayson. I have to go."

"And whose fault is that? You left and you kept our son from me! You could have had all this! You could have had it and you threw it away!" I'm yelling and I know I might wake Max but I can't bring myself to care.

Lillian's still crying but her mouth is set in a hard line. "I already apologized, but I know a life time of apologies will never make up for that. But I'll say it again, Grayson, I am sorry I didn't tell you about your son. I had my reasons to leave, but keeping you from Max was wrong." She is shaking her head. She whispers, "Now, please, if you hate me so much, Grayson, then why won't you let me go?"

"I can't," I say hoarsely, and Lillian bites her lip and starts to put the clothes back in her bag.

Suddenly, I'm back to that place all over again. I'm back to where I was before, when she left, and I can't tell which way is up. I feel exhausted and heartbroken and all I can do is watch her when she leaves, rolling her bag behind her and shutting the front door.

It sounds like the end of the world.

34

LILLIAN

God, I hope Max hasn't woken up during the screaming match that we just had. I know it will be hard to explain to him, but I have to leave for a few days. I can't do this anymore, especially with a new baby coming.

I have to quit my new job, and that's a shame because despite having gotten it because of Grayson, I really love it. My presentation about Breckwood Textiles had gone so well. Now I would be looking for jobs at some greasy spoon diner or maybe a bartending gig at a dive bar. Having my degree is all well and good, but when I need quick money, I have to work more menial jobs.

I don't want to quit over the phone, and my laptop contains a lot of recent pictures and videos of Max, so I drive to the office, wiping at my face in the parking lot.

Truth is, I don't ever want to come back here. I can't face Grayson, and Mallory is someone I have no interest of ever seeing again, no matter what the future brings.

Might as well go now, when I won't have to explain myself to anyone, since the office will be empty.

And though I'll miss Meredith, who has become a real

friend to me, I just can't do this anymore, not after Grayson has been so kind to me with my pregnancy symptoms. He has no idea it's because I'm growing his baby in my belly, and it's making me nuts that I can be with him but not *be* with him. Not in the way I want.

It's late and no one is in the office, thank God, so I unlock my office door and walk inside, letting out a shaky breath.

"What are you doing here?" The voice seems to come from nowhere, and I squeeze my eyes shut, recognizing it.

"Hello, Mallory," I say flatly, and when I turn to look at her she's standing in the doorway, frowning.

"What are you doing here so late? You don't plan to try and steal something, do you?"

I roll my eyes, no longer caring to be polite.

"Just getting my things," I say. "What are *you* doing here?"

Mallory shrugs. "Not that it's any of your business, this is my husband's company, but Meredith and I went to dinner and she forgot her briefcase."

I hum, not wanting to make small talk and packing up my things.

Mallory keeps standing in the doorway, looking at me suspiciously, and I ignore her.

"I suppose we've gotten off on the wrong foot, Lillian," she says, and I'm so surprised that I nearly drop my laptop as I put it into my bag.

"That's an understatement," I mutter.

"Can't we let the past be the past? Bygones be bygones?"

I stare at her. "No. We can't. And you hate me, so why would you want to make peace now?"

Mallory sighs. "Because of my grandson. I don't know

how you managed to raise such an amazing kid, but I love him dearly and I don't want any bad blood between us."

I swallow hard. I want Max to have as many people in his life that love him as possible, but I don't think I can deal with being friends with Mallory Whitlock.

"So, you're saying I should forgive you?"

Mallory keeps her blue eyes trained on my face. "I think we should forgive each other," she says tightly.

I let out a long breath, anger rising in me. "I have done absolutely nothing to be forgiven for,"

35

GRAYSON

I lost it when she left, wanting to throw everything in my room, but I didn't, going to Holly's room and telling her that she needed to keep an eye on Max while I left.

When there's no one listed under either Lillian Brooks or Lillian Whitlock anywhere, I got back into the car, slamming the steering wheel over and over again and yelling, full of anger and pain.

She did it again. She left me all over again.

I can't handle it, and I have to go after her. The first person I think of is Maria, her best friend, but I don't have her number and I want to explore a few other avenues before hopping on a plane to New York. Maybe she's gone to the office, gotten her things, and quit. Lillian is good at disappearing, after all. She knows how to do it and how to do it well. The years that I searched for her prove that.

As I walk up to her office building, I see my mother's BMW in the parking lot and I groan. I don't want to deal with Mallory Whitlock today, but I guess I'm going to have to. When I round the corner, my mother is standing in Lillian's doorway.

I freeze, wondering what they could possibly be talking about. Was Mom trying to talk her out of it? They have seemed to be at odds ever since the wedding so they weren't exactly chummy.

"I have done absolutely nothing to be forgiven for!" Lillian burst out.

I pause again after taking a few more steps, hearing her words. What are they even talking about? As far as I know, they barely know each other. I know eavesdropping is wrong but I still don't know why Lillian left, so I listen to the rest of the conversation, hiding behind one of the columns.

"Haven't you? You left, didn't you?" my mother asks, and I know she's trying to take up for me. The next thing that Lillian says rocks me to my core.

"You made sure of it, didn't you?"

My heart does jumping jacks in my chest. Made sure of *what*? Surely, my mother would never... But I know Mallory Whitlock.

"All I did was point the truth out to you. Ultimately, you made the decision," my mother says. "When you blame me for all your problems, maybe you should think about that."

"Get out of my office," Lillian sounds angry, and my head is spinning. Could this be the reason she left? Was it my own mother all along?

"Just remember. You made your own choices."

The click of my mother's heels on the hardwood floors sounds too loud as she strides by me, and I catch up to her in a couple of long-legged strides, grabbing her arm and pulling her into one of the offices nearby.

My mother's eyes, blue just like mine, widen in shock.

"Grayson? What are you doing here?"

"What the hell did you do?" I ask, my voice low and rasping from all the emotion I've been through this morning. All the emotion I've been through because of my own mother, the woman who was supposed to love me before all else.

She swallows. "I don't know what you're talking about."

I release my grip on her arm because I'm angry and I don't want to hurt her. I draw in a sharp breath, feeling like I'm going to break apart any second.

"I heard you talking to Lillian," I accuse, and something flashes across her face before she shuts it down all over again. She's good at that. She taught me to be good at it, too, and maybe that's how I got in this mess in the first place.

"You must have misheard," she says innocently, and I grit my teeth so hard my jaw aches.

"What the hell did you say to her?"

She blinks as if confused, and as much as I love my mother, I hate her just as much in this instant.

"I just told her the truth, Grayson," she says, as if she actually believes that.

"What truth? You don't know my truth, Mother," I snarl.

"You don't understand how the world works, Grayson," she sighs. "You never did. It's my fault. I coddled you too much."

"Just the way you're coddling me now? Not telling me what the hell you said to my *wife.*"

"She wasn't your wife then," she snaps, and then clamps a hand over her mouth like she didn't mean to say that.

I stare at her for a long moment. "You did this."

"She made her choices, Grayson! I just... gave her all the options," she pleads, taking a step toward me.

I step back. If she touches me right now, I don't know what I'll do.

"You ruined my *life,*" I say quietly, and my mother scoffs.

"I *protected* you. Look at what she's doing now, leaving all over again! She's not for you, Grayson."

"Get out of here, Mother. We'll talk about this later." My voice is quiet and calm, but I'm raging inside.

I start to stride off, knowing that I'll lose it if I don't, and I have more important things to do right now. I need to find Lillian, and *now*. Just like I told my mother, she ruined my life five years ago and I'm not about to let her do it again.

"Grayson, wait!" my mother sobs, turning on the waterworks, but I ignore her.

36

LILLIAN

"Get out of my office," I snap.

Mallory smiles and it's an empty, vicious smile. "Just remember. You made your own choices."

I refuse to look at her face a single second longer, because I might be tempted to just slap her silly.

She finally walks out and I wait a few moments, breathing hard, until she must be out of the building. I have to run to throw up again on the way out, and it gives me a headache.

As soon as I get inside the safety of my car, I take a deep breath. This day is never-ending. I just want to hide under the covers and wake up months from now. Gathering the last bit of strength still inside me, I head to the only hotel I can afford in the area—a motel off the interstate that's about thirty miles from Grayson's mansion.

Grayson... I'm deeply in love with him, and I can't deny that to myself any longer. I need to get away before I lose my mind, and this motel is the only way to do it.

I'm sobbing when I pull into the parking garage, and I take a long moment to pull myself together before I go in and check into the hotel. The elevator is out and I have to take the stairs to the third floor and it feels like I've walked miles.

I wasn't this tired when I was pregnant with Max, I swear. I don't know what it is about this baby, but it's making me exhausted. It was all I could do to get through my presentation today, and after the night I had, all I want to do is sleep.

After about an hour of sleep, my phone starts buzzing, but there's no text saying that the call is from Max so I don't answer. I don't know why he's calling me, anyway. Grayson doesn't love me, he's made that abundantly clear. Maybe he used to. I don't know anymore. I thought I did. I thought I knew that things were casual, but I guess I might have been wrong, from what Grayson told me.

It still doesn't feel real, that I've left, and I miss Max terribly already even though he's just thirty miles away and safe with his father. I don't know how to do this, to be away from my son, but if I don't get a few days' rest, my body is going to give out.

I don't know how to continue to do this with Grayson. I know I need to face him sooner or later, even if just because of Max and to tell him he is going to be a father again, but right now I can't even stomach that idea.

I call Maria, needing to talk to *somebody*, and Maria answers on the third ring.

I start sobbing as soon as I hear her voice.

"Lillian, what's wrong?" she asks, concerned. "Is it the new baby?"

"No, no, nothing like that," I sob. "I asked Grayson for a divorce."

"*What*? I thought you were dedicated to... whatever it was you two had going on."

"I thought I was too," I say honestly, "but with the new baby, everything's changed."

"What's changed, Lillian? You were set to raise Max in a marriage of convenience or whatever—"

"What's changed is I'm in love with him," I burst out, and then a fresh set of tears begins to fall.

"Of course you're in love with him, honey. He's in love with you too," she insists.

"No, he isn't. He hates me because I left with Max, and who could blame him? I just wish that I'd never done this."

"If you'd never done it, you would have never realized that you could be in love like this, Lil."

"It doesn't matter if he doesn't love me *back*, Maria," I sniffle, and she sighs.

"He's being an idiot. I know he loves you. I saw the way he looks at you."

"You don't understand," I tell her. "He wants my body, but not me. It's not me he wants."

"It's going to be okay, Lillian. Where are you? I'll come get you and Max, bring you back to New York if I have to."

"No, I can't do that. I can't take Max out of state, Maria, Grayson will take him from me," I say quickly. "Besides, I already made that mistake once, I'm not going to do it again."

"Okay, okay. I'll stand by, just in case. You disappeared once, you can do it again."

I bite my lip. I wish I could disappear. I wish I could leave and never come back, that I'd never come back at all, but now that I'd seen Max with Grayson, I couldn't do it. I couldn't take him from his father that he loves so much. And I couldn't do to this baby what I had done to Max. It had been bad enough doing it once.

"Max doesn't deserve to lose his father, and the baby...

He needs a father too. I won't be that cruel again," I say softly, and Maria's quiet for a long moment on the other line.

"I don't know what to do to help you, Lillian. Tell me what to do," she pleads, and I feel such a surge of love for her I wish I could hug her. She's my best friend for a reason, after all, and it's because she has such a big heart.

"I just needed a friendly ear, that's all. Just to vent a bit and take this out of my chest. But I'll be okay," I tell her. "I promise. I just need to get some rest. This baby is making me so tired."

"Okay, if you say so. Please call me if you need me, okay?"

"I will. I promise."

We hang up and I plop down on the bed on my back, letting tears fall from the corners of my eyes.

There's nothing that I can do now except waiting until my heart stops aching so much. It was like this before, when I left, and I had thought that I'd never get any better. I'd thought that it'd go on hurting forever, and I guess it had.

I cry myself to sleep, and ignore the buzzing of my phone.

When I wake, I'm disoriented, used to being in Grayson's house, and I look at my watch to see that it's after midnight. I haven't slept more than a couple of hours, unfortunately. I want to sleep until I feel better, until my heartache is healed more, but it doesn't look like that's going to happen.

There's a knock at my motel door, and I startle. This isn't the best side of town, after all, and I'm a woman alone.

"Who is it?" I call weakly.

"Grayson," he barks, and I groan out loud.

I walk to the door and look through the peephole.

"Go away, Grayson," I tell him.

"If you want me to leave, you're going to have to call the cops," he says, and I sigh and open the door.

"I'm not coming back," I say as soon as he walks in the door.

Grayson nods. His eyes are bloodshot, probably from drinking.

"I'm not here to ask you to come back," he says, wiping a hand across his face. His bright blue eyes are wet, and I'm shocked by it.

"Then why are you here?" I ask quietly as he shuts the door. I back up against the bed.

"Because once and for all, I need you to tell me the truth about why you left me five years ago."

37

GRAYSON

After the talk with my mother I went back to Lilian's office, but she was no longer there.

It had taken me hours to find her. I knew how much she made, and she could have probably stayed at one of the more expensive hotels, but I also knew that she wouldn't. I know Lillian, and she's not comfortable staying in places like that. She wasn't even comfortable in our hotel room that we had for the honeymoon, what little of it there was.

As soon as that front door closed after our fight, I wanted to throw everything in my room, but I didn't. I couldn't handle her absence, the void she had left behind. I had to go after her.

I had to know why.

But of all the reasons that I'd thought she'd left, this is the absolute last one I would have thought of.

"Tell me everything," I plead. I'm tired of this shit and I really need to know what the hell happened five years ago.

"I don't want to hurt you, Grayson. Please, let it go." She sighs. She looks exhausted.

"No, I really need to know. I heard you and my mother at

the office tonight. Please, Lil." I'm begging now. I need to be sure. I need to know.

She shakes her head and tells me, "Your mother, the woman who just recently asked me to divorce you, first came to see me five years ago." She is talking quietly.

"And what, she offered to pay you off?" I ask. "You took the money to leave me?" I hate the thought of that almost more than Lillian leaving of her own accord.

"God, no!" Lillian cries. "She offered, yes, asked me what my price was, but I didn't take a cent from her. Not now, not ever. But back then, she found me at my second job, the waitressing one? She came to my *work*, Grayson, same as she does now. That day, she pulled me into a booth when I started my break and told me all of the reasons that I should get out of town. Without you."

"And what reasons were that?" I ask, sitting down heavily on the other double bed in the room. "What possible reasons could you have to just leave like that?"

"She showed me I wasn't good enough for you, Grayson. She told me I was just a poor girl from the wrong side of the tracks, that everyone would know I wanted you for your money. She said I'd be a dark spot on your future, that people would know I was a phony." Tears are silently streaming down her eyes as her voice slightly wavers but doesn't falter. "For hours, she reminded me of who I was and who you were and how much I was fooling myself if I thought I was anything more than a bed warmer to you. She told me I was one in many, but none of us meant nothing to you. She showed me I was better off leaving."

Her eyes move to her hands on her lap. "You see, I always knew that I'm not good enough for you." She nearly whispers the last part, and it makes my heart ache.

I lean forward, my heart doing some kind of flip in my

chest. Is this true? Because if it is, this means that Lillian didn't leave me for someone else, didn't leave me because she didn't love me...

"You broke me, Lillian. You leaving almost killed me," I say hoarsely. "And I hated you for it. So much." I see her recoil from my words, but she needs to hear this. It's important she understands. So, I hold her hand in both of mine and force her to look at me, so she can see the truth in my words. "But the worst part was that I hated me most of all. Because no matter how much you hurt me when you left, and even after I found out what you took from me, all this time, I've been fighting my feelings for you because you're so wonderful. And I couldn't let myself love you anymore, because then you could destroy me again. Just as you did five years ago."

"I didn't mean to," she says, tears choking her voice. "I didn't know that you loved me. You never said anything..."

I take her other hand in mine too, squeezing them both. "I loved you so much." I pause, and I'm afraid to say what I'm going to say next but I have to say it, have to tell her. "I still love you so much."

Lillian lets out a sob and pulls away from me. "Don't say that. Don't say that, Grayson. You can't say that if it's not true."

"It is true," I insist, leaning forward to take her hands again, and she lets me. "It's true, I fell back in love with you so quickly it scared me. The way you are with Max, the way you are at work... You're everything, Lillian. You always have been."

"You can't say that if you don't mean it, Grayson," she says again, and I lean forward and kiss her, putting everything I feel into it. All the pain, all the love that I've been hiding, and she sobs into my mouth.

"Do you believe me now?" I ask, tears streaming down my face as I look at her, and Lillian puts her hand on my cheek, crying.

"Really? You really want me? Even though I'm different than you? Even though I'm so much less…"

"You are not less. You are everything. And the fact that you are different is *why* I want you, Lillian. You give me everything I need, everything I'm lacking. And you've grown into such a wonderful mother…"

"What about your mother?" Lillian asks, as if my words reminded her.

I'm quiet for a long moment. "Fuck my mother," I growl. "She has a lot to answer for."

"Grayson, you can't say that. What about your family?"

"I found my family. I stumbled across you and Max while I was on business and I never want to let either of you go."

"Grayson," she cries, and climbs into my lap, and I kiss her.

Lillian pushes me away, and I'm crestfallen until she holds a hand over her mouth.

"Are you still sick?" I ask her, concerned. "Do we need to go to the hospital? You've been sick a while now, Lillian—"

She puts a hand to her belly and I just frown, tilting my head.

"I'm gonna be sick a while longer. I'm pregnant, Grayson."

My head feels like it's going to explode with all the new information I've learned tonight, but this time, I'm happy, my heart soaring.

"Really?" I put a hand over hers on her stomach. "A baby? One that I can watch learn to walk?" Tears spring to my eyes again, and I swear this is the most I've cried since I was a little kid.

She smiles. "Really, Grayson. I'm having your baby all over again."

"Fuck me," I say, and then cover my mouth with my hand. "I'm going to have to work on that."

Lillian giggles. "We'll get a swear jar." Looking at me straight in the eye, she adds, "I'm sorry I had to get out of the house. I just needed a little time and space because I was too overwhelmed, but I'd never keep this from you. I learned from my mistake."

"I can understand that. Especially now that I finally know the truth."

"I also wanted to tell you something. One of the few things I brought with me was Max's baby photo albums. I have pictures and videos of him since he was born, if you want to look at them?"

"You do?" This means I can maybe still witness some of those moments of Max, even if a bit differently. But it would mean the world to me having that piece of him be a part of me.

She nods. "I do. I wanted to tell you from the start but you always seemed to not want to talk to me or always be mad at me, and I never really got around to asking you because I was always afraid of making things worse. I'm sorry. But we can just go through them whenever you want."

"Whenever I want?" I challenge.

"Yes, whenever you want." She smiles at me.

"Fuck, yes." My hand goes to my mouth again. I really have to work on that.

"We're definitely getting a swear jar." She laughs.

I search her face. "Does that mean you'll come back? Be my wife? For real this time?"

She bites her lip like she does when she's unsure. "If... if you want me to. If you're ready for that."

"I'm ready for that," I say easily. "But we'll have to do it again. Right, this time."

"I don't think my dress held up from last time," she jokes, and I laugh through my tears, cradling her in my arms.

"We'll buy you a new one. Anything you want."

"A new ring, too?" she asks, and I shake my head, frowning.

"No, the same ring. I bought that for you five years ago."

Lillian gasps. "You didn't."

"I did." I grin at her. "I've been gone for you since the first time I saw you. I told my mother I was going to marry you. I guess that's why she found you."

"Grayson," she says, her voice trembling. "Why didn't you tell me? Why didn't you tell me how you felt, back then?"

I shrug. "I was going to. I was going to tell you everything and propose to you, but then you just... you left."

"I didn't know," she sobs. "I swear to you I didn't know. I thought that you were just playing with me."

"I would never do that," I promise her. "I would never play with your feelings like that."

Lillian scoffs but her brown eyes are sparkling. "That's all you've been doing since I came back."

I bark out a laugh. "I'm sorry. I was just so angry that you left. You're the only woman I've ever loved, sweetheart. You know that, don't you?"

"I do now," she says, and she kisses me.

When we make love, it's nothing like the last time. It's real, and it's right, and I'm home.

38

GRAYSON

I stand outside my mother's mansion, hesitating before ringing the doorbell. I'm here for a reason and I can't pull it off any longer. Just knowing that this woman, my own mother, is the reason that I didn't witness my son's birth. My son's firsts. She purposefully caused my unnecessary suffering for the past five years... She consoled me without ever even hinting at her role in any of it. She never even showed any kind of regret for making me hurt so much.

I knew she was cold, but not that cold.

I've always known my mother wouldn't approve of Lilian because of where she came from, but this is too sinister. It's a step too far, even for her.

Taking a deep breath, I ring the doorbell and wait. I don't belong here anymore. I think I never really did.

When she opens, surprise colors her face. "Grayson, what are you doing here?"

"We need to talk," I try to keep my anger in check.

"Of course, come in." She steps aside.

I follow her into the living room and sit down on the couch opposite her. "Let's cut to the chase, shall we? I'm going to ask you a question and I need you to tell me the truth."

She nods at me, suspicion and cunning all over her now slightly squinted eyes. She is smiling but it's forced. "Of course."

"Why did you tell Lilian to leave me?"

My mother looks away, clearly uncomfortable. "I don't know why we have to go through this again," she says.

"Answer me, Mother." My anger starting to boil over. "I know you went to her work. You're the one who made her leave. Why would you do that? You knew I was going to ask her to marry me. You knew I loved her."

She hesitates for a moment before finally admitting the truth. "Yes, I sent her away. She was beneath you. Unworthy. But believe me when I tell you I didn't know she was pregnant, otherwise I would have handled things differently."

"You had no right to meddle in the first place. This wasn't your life, it was mine. And because of you, I missed my son's first years of life, and for five years, I was miserable. What kind of mother does that to their child? Harms them so much they break them inside?" I ask, my heart racing.

"She would have ruined your future. I couldn't let that happen, so I made her leave. But I didn't know about Max, I swear. I'm not sorry I made her go, she wasn't right for you. Still isn't. I'm just sorry because Max shouldn't have been stuck with her. He should have been here, being raised as the Whitlock he is. But, Grayson, my son, we still have time. You can divorce her now and..."

She might as well have punched me in the stomach. This woman is heartless. "Divorce her? I love her, why would I divorce her?"

"Because she isn't a good fit for you. Did she even tell you she is pregnant? Because she is. And that baby and Max need to have the right upbringing. They have to learn what being a Whitlock really is. They don't need to be around someone so—"

"Stop!" I stand up from the couch, anger and hurt giving way to a feeling of emptiness. "When I found out, I had my doubts that you could be so evil, so selfish. I didn't want to face the truth I see before me now. You are a petty, bitter woman who never knew love, so you begrudge your own son for loving and being loved, and you don't stop until he is the spitting image of you." My voice is shaking. "But guess what. You get your wish after all, Mother."

She looks at me with a hopeful gleam in her eye. "You *are* divorcing her? You don't have to worry about a thing. I'll contact our lawyers because of the childr—"

"No, I'm not." How could she even think that? I just told her I love Lilian. How rotten can this woman be? "If I have my say, I'll never let Lilian go. But you never have to see her again. In fact, you'll never have to see any of us again."

"Grayson, what are you talking about?"

I look her right in the eye and my voice drops to a low, threatening tone. "Don't you *ever* come near my family again. You are no longer a part of it, and I never want to see you again. I hope you are happy now. Have a nice life."

Without another word, I walk out of the mansion, leaving the woman I now realize was just my mother in name. Now that I see how Lilian treats Max, I see what a mother really is supposed to be like, I can clearly see Mallory Whitlock is not it.

I still can't believe my own mother could be capable of such betrayal.

I left Lilian at our home to unpack, and I can't wait to go back to her.

As I walk down the driveway, I'm hit by all the missed

opportunities and lost time. I can't change the past, but I can try to make up for it in the present. I get into my car and set off to find the woman I love. Leaving my hurtful past behind me, I now look forward to a loving future. With her. With Max. With this new baby that is coming. My family.

The drive home is long and emotional. A cocktail of emotions, anger, sadness, and regret swirls inside me. I think of all Lilian and Max had to go through because of my mother's selfishness.

As I finally arrive, I open the door and immediately go to her. Her look shows her shock as well as her delight at seeing him back so soon. I told her I had to leave, but I didn't tell her why or when I was coming back.

"Grayson, back already?" Her smile warms me up inside. I go to her, putting my hands on her hips.

"I couldn't stay away for long. I don't think I'll ever let you out of my sight again." I kiss her tenderly for a second. "But I had to go talk to my mother."

She looks at me for a second or two and lowers her eyes to my chest. "How did that go?" Tears well up in her beautiful eyes. I never want her to shed another sad tear again. And I'll do everything in my power to make sure of it from now on.

"I told her she is no longer part of my family and she would never see any of us again."

Her eyes rise to meet mine, a few tears have escaped down her face. "You don't have to do that, Gray. She's your mother, after all. Let's just make sure her path and mine don't cross. I've had my fair share of her already, to last me for life, actually."

"I love you, Lil, and I want to make things right. And that includes separating from a toxic woman who never really loved me for me. She loves money and power more than anything else, so she can have those and leave us alone. We don't need her or her venom in our family."

She steps forward and wraps her arms around me. "I've never stopped loving you, you know?" she says, her voice choked with tears. "Not really."

I hold her close, a sense of relief washing over me. There is still a lot to work through, but I am determined to make things right and start a new future together. It won't be easy, but with Lilian by my side, I can face anything.

We pull away from each other, and I look deep into Lilian's eyes. My voice filled with emotion, I tell her, "You and our children are all I ever want. My family. *Our* family."

Lilian nods, tears streaming down her face. "Our family," she says. "I want to spend the rest of my life with you, Grayson. That was true five years ago, and it still is."

I lean down and kiss her, sealing our promise of a new life together.

As our lips touch, I know I found my way home.

39

LILLIAN

I'm nine months pregnant before we're able to get married, again, and I'm wearing what appears to be a tent when I'm not wearing it, a huge maternity dress that fits me well when I put it on.

It's not as extravagant as the last dress, with several thousand less dollars on the price tag, but it's what I want. It still has a sweetheart neckline, and Grayson still looks at me like he wants to eat me alive when I walk down the aisle.

This time, though, that's not all that's in his blue eyes. There's love there, too, and Max is standing next to him, his suit just like his daddy's, and grinning. He's more than excited to meet his baby sister.

We didn't bother to get divorced, thinking that it would be silly, so we just did a renewing of our vows, and it's lovely. Meredith is still in my bridal party, and it's still Grayson's father who walks me down the aisle. Maria's my maid of honor, and she's so excited to be there she can barely stand it. The only person missing was Mallory. She had not been invited at all.

I go into labor on our wedding night, which we spend at

home in our penthouse apartment, one that Grayson paid for with his own money and not from his parents. We've both left Whitlock because we wanted to distance ourselves as much as possible from the toxicity that meant having Mallory around.

"Are you sure?" Grayson asks, running around to get the bag we had packed, his blue eyes wide. He's been lovely throughout my pregnancy, waiting on me hand and foot and making me breakfast every morning—lots of meat products because it turns out the baby is a carnivore, too.

"I'm sure," I say, looking down at the puddle of water in the bed. "My water just broke."

"Fuck!" he cries, and Max giggles.

"Swear jar, Daddy," he says, and Grayson pulls out his wallet and places a bill into the jar. It's filled with twenties from Grayson's cursing.

I laugh too, but it turns into a groan when a contraction rips through me.

"We gotta go," he tells Max, and Holly comes out of her room. She stayed with us after we left Los Angeles and moved to Oakland, and she's lovely with Max as usual.

Grayson's starting his own advertising business, and I'm going to be the main executive, among others, like Derek, who decided to take a chance on his childhood friend. Grayson doesn't want anything to do with his family's money, and I can't blame him.

We still allow Max to visit his aunt and grandfather, but Mallory has been cut off. Max misses her a bit, and I wonder if some day maybe we can forgive each other, but for now, Grayson's still upset.

I understand. We were kept apart for so long because of her and because of my own insecurities. He missed out on Max's life, and I know how much that hurts him.

He's gone to every doctor's appointment for the new baby, who we've yet to name. We just can't seem to decide.

Grayson wants to name her after me, but I don't like the idea of a Lillian, Jr, so we haven't made up our minds. Since she'll be here in a few hours, I figure we need to.

Labor goes by slow as Christmas it seems, although baby girl seemed to want to be out early. My due date isn't until next week, after all. It's not as painful as it was with Max, though, because Grayson's right there, holding my hand while I yell in pain and rubbing my back when I start to cry.

It's too late for an epidural so I have to suffer for about five hours before I finally give birth, and stars are in Grayson's eyes already when he looks down at her.

"She looks like a Kylie, to me," I say, thinking of one of the baby names that I'd seen in a book.

"Kylie," Grayson says in wonder, and when she puts her little fist around his thumb, he bursts into tears.

I start crying too, thinking this is what he missed with Max, this is everything that he needed to have from the beginning.

They allow me to go home the next day, and Grayson's exhausted, having barely slept on the chairs in the hospital, refusing to leave me for more than a few hours. Back at home, when Max meets her, he holds out his arms.

"Baby, please," he says politely, and I laugh.

"Her name is Kylie," Grayson tells him, and Max sounds out her name softly.

"Kylie," he says. "My sister."

"Your little sister," Grayson says. "I've got one of those too, your Aunt Meredith, and she's a pain in my butt, but I love her and I'll always protect her."

Max nods in wonder and I make him sit down on the couch, wincing a little as I sit down next to him. When

Grayson puts Kylie in his arms, she's fussing, but she stops, seeming awed by her big brother's face, when Max holds her.

He's gentle just like he should be, and Grayson looks at me with tears in his blue eyes.

"Lillian," he says. "We have a real family now."

"Yes, we do," I say, and when he kisses me, it's like all the years we weren't together are gone, and like we've been home all along, we just didn't know it.

ALSO BY CALLIE STEVENS

Spades Brothers Series

Accidental Baby For My Brother's Best Friend

Accidental Secret Daddy

Secret Baby For My Best Friends Brother

Baby For My Best Friend's Ex

Soul Sounds Brothers

Stuck With My Rockstar Boss

Unexpected Baby For My Brother's Best Friend

Accidental Fake Fiancé

Claimed By My Best Friend's Brother

The Hawthorns Series

Baby For Daddy's Best Friend

Baby For The Off Limits Single Daddy

Secret Daddy Next Door

Baby For The Off Limits Boss Daddy

Alpha Billionaire Daddies

Damaged Secret Daddy

Fake Fiancé Boss Daddy

Broken Single Daddy's Baby